Glassman, Maxine.

Love among the orientals.

| DATE | | | |
|---|---|---|---|
| | | | |
| | | | |
| | | | |
| | | | |
| | | | |
| | | | |
| | | | |
| | | | |
| | | | |
| | | | |
| | | | |
| | | | |

# Love Among the Orientals

# Love Among the Orientals

Maxine Glassman

Donald I. Fine Books
New York

DONALD I. FINE BOOKS
Published by the Penguin Group
Penguin Putnam Inc., 375 Hudson Street,
New York, New York 10014, U.S.A.
Penguin Books Ltd, 27 Wrights Lane, London W8 5TZ, England
Penguin Books Australia Ltd, Ringwood, Victoria, Australia
Penguin Books Canada Ltd, 10 Alcorn Avenue,
Toronto, Ontario, Canada M4V 3B2
Penguin Books (N.Z.) Ltd, 182–190 Wairau Road,
Auckland 10, New Zealand

Penguin Books Ltd, Registered Offices: Harmondsworth, Middlesex, England

First published by Donald I. Fine Books, an imprint of Penguin Putnam Inc.

First Printing, June, 1998
10 9 8 7 6 5 4 3 2 1



Library of Congress Cataloging-in-Publication Data is available.

Printed in the United States of America
Set in Garamond Light

PUBLISHER'S NOTE
This is a work of fiction. Names, characters, places, and incidents either are the products of the author's imagination or are used fictitiously, and any resemblance to actual persons, living or dead, events, or locales is entirely coincidental.

*For Bruce*

Like great poems, Oriental rugs release powerful emotions and truths in an expression whose impact is both personal and immediate.

Some of the most pervasive and insistent messages contained in Oriental rugs deal with sex.

—*The Lost Language*
John M. Douglass and Sue N. Peters

# Love Among the Orientals

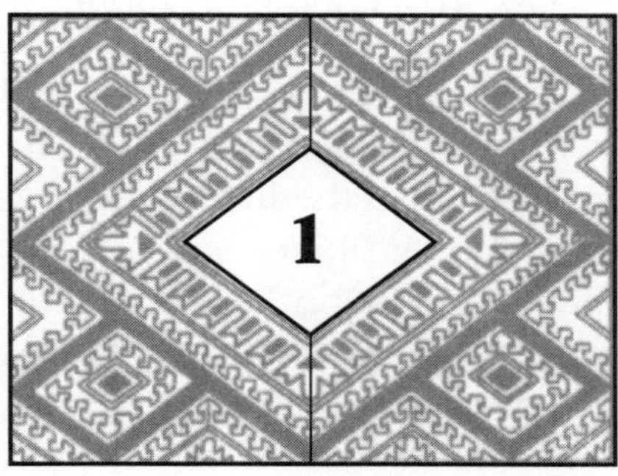

X-rated, that's what it should have been. An ordinary storefront on Boylston Street, in the heart of Boston's Back Bay. Flanked by an art gallery to the left and a native American craft store to the right, Classic Design was deceptively unpretentious. An Oriental rug store, its glinting windows hung with an array of bold and colorful rugs. Not quite. Something else.

Owned and operated by Jake and Doris Seagull, it seemed to be the quintessential ma-and-pa endeavor. Small potatoes, but such an attitude! Ma Doris, an independently wealthy (big inheritance) and high-strung woman, had a great eye for rugs. And she was smart. Pa Jake, who knew who was buttering his croissants and did daily obeisance, took care of business.

Contrary to other purveyors of fine Persian carpets, the Seagulls had done their best to dispel the aura of magic and mystery that usually surrounded the merchandise. No dark Mediterranean salespeople lurked in the shadows. The store was well lit. No mumbo jumbo, no haggling, no bargains. Women, rarely seen in the souks and bazaars of the Middle East, or in any other local rug store, ruled the roost. The concept of the Oriental rug as a decorative necessity, like a sofa or a chair, had paid off handsomely. Only the staff had succumbed to the romance of the rugs and behaved accordingly. The constant proximity to the lush floor coverings had, some would say, affected their libidos.

Be it the poor ventilation intermingling with the heavy wool of the imported carpets, there hovered over this rug store a translucent cloud of rarefied air. Or blame the rich, glowing colors intricately woven into provocatively appealing shapes. That, coupled with the oppressive air, could be what was affecting all who labored at Classic Design.

Beyond the realm of reason, there was another consideration. It was the spell cast upon the rugs by one Achmed Asher. Asher was the customs broker who facilitated the entry of the rugs through the port of Boston for Jake Seagull. Years ago the two men had a serious clash, and although their differences had long since been resolved, the weird incantation conceived and chanted during that awkward period had survived. Call it poor sportsmanship or hard feelings, Achmed's hex, a bit of doggerel loosely derived from the *Kama Sutra,* the classic Indian textbook on erotica, was still invoked over every single shipment to Classic Design. (Achmed was a firm believer in the *Kama Sutra.*) It went something like this:

Let all who touch these rugs of treasure
Be roused to heights of sexual pleasure.
The mind will fog, the body ache
All because I don't trust you, Jake.

In all probability, discounting that bizarre glitch, there was a logical scientific explanation for the inherent carnal phenomenon. Nobody knew what it was, but the special pleasure of working at CD did exact its toll.

There wasn't much doing in the rug store, the chief hazard of the trade. There didn't have to be. Two or three good sales per day, and business was booming. To avoid the inertia brought on by the sluggish pace, the employees pooled their creative talents to provide diversion. Otherwise they'd go nuts.

Luckily for the help, there was always a full crew aboard. Ma Doris knew her business, and she insisted upon it. If one person couldn't conjure up the perfect rug for a client, the next person gave it a shot. Staff did not work on commission. Sometimes it took a group effort. Customers responded in a very positive manner to all the attention. It was an effective ploy.

Oddly enough the Seagulls believed themselves to be overworked. Truth was, they spent most of the year away from the store: Florida in the winter and spring, Connecticut in the summer. Their reigning passions were golf and tennis. Much time, effort, and money (for lessons and club memberships) were spent in perfecting their strokes and swings. Doris thought she was a better athlete than Jake, and that was a little problem. They were very competitive. (In fact, eight times out of ten, Jake let Doris beat him. It was a game plan calculated to keep her happy. Jake was committed to keeping Doris happy.) Whatever, they were dependent on a steadfast and loyal staff. They chose their people carefully. Ergo, most of the staff was overqualified. But the Seagulls paid well, and money, after all, was the bottom line.

Every morning, six days a week, Classic Design opened for business. Not like clockwork and not always at 9:30, the designated hour. Only the top two trusted employees enjoyed key privileges. They took turns opening. There was an assortment of locks, bolts, padlocks, and alarms to negotiate. (Ma Doris was paranoid.) Invariably, the phone was ringing: Jake, wherever he was, checking on his help. The staff, commuters all, having been hassled in heavy traffic or worse, arrived at the last moment, huffing and puffing and grumbling and fumbling with keys and brown-bagged lunches. Then, voila, the lights were switched on and CD was in business.

It was a great big, cavernous store. The walls were paneled oak. The floor was a honey-colored hardwood. Overhead, scores of spotlights in a tight geometric grid beamed down on the merchandise. The place was literally crammed with rugs: on the walls, on the floor, rolled up, stacked up, hung up. Everywhere. Midway against one lateral wall, there were two old, oversized oak rolltop desks with four unmatched wooden chairs. An assortment of filing cabinets attended the desks. This was the heart of the operation. No frills.

Sophie did the key tricks this day. Having seniority both in age and in years of employment, she was everybody's favorite, an earth mother type. An attractive, ageless, and spry small brunette (bottled, probably), she often dressed to suit her mood. Today, clad in a straight black skirt topped by a colorfully embroidered Mexican shirt, and sporting long turquoise and silver Navajo earrings, she was obviously in good spirits.

Jon, Lesley, and Sarah jostled past Sophie, who was standing by the desks, already talking on the phone to Jake. They shed their coats, dumped their lunches in the small fridge at the back, and headed for their appointed places. The two apprentice rug handlers/shippers straggled in. Show and Tell was the first order of the day. They were all great talkers. But not before coffee. One of the rug schleppers volunteered to fetch coffee, bless him.

An attractive young woman wandered in. Although CD was supposedly under alarmed lock and key, and a customer had to ring to be allowed entrance, the door was usually left wide open to let air circulate around the heavy, hairy inventory, which the staff believed was robbing them of an ozone layer. In other words, it was hard to breathe in Classic Design. The front door was the only means of egress. There were no windows, no back door. No one liked to think about it.

The woman roamed about. Four sets of antennae zoomed up. Lesley got up from the desk and asked if she might be of help. "Not really, I just want to see what you have." Lesley trailed the potential customer, explaining where the different rugs were placed. Lesley, a longtime employee, had the gift. She knew how to work an uninterested browser into an enthusiastic tryer-outer. She was good and she had the floor.

Show and Tell resumed sans Lesley. Sophie had attended a performance of Leonard Bernstein's *Candide* at the

Huntington Theater. She did a brief recap, adding her own unique observations, and called for a discussion. Jon, an amateur thespian, was resident theater critic. (He'd appeared in numerous suburban productions.) Before he could expound on *Candide,* the phone rang. It was Jake again. He said he'd be late, he was working at home. Next a call for Lesley. She left her customer for a brief spell. She covered the mouthpiece of the phone as she spoke, but there was no help, no privacy. It was her special friend, and he wanted to see her today. She perked right up, color rushing to her cheeks. Sophie, Jon, and Sarah tried to look busy. In a few minutes, Lesley, rosy and smiling, was back on the job, beguiling her prospective client.

Jon Hedstrom had a problem. Crisis at home. So what else was new? Tall, handsome Jon, nattily attired in a navy blazer, gray flannels, and a maroon paisley silk ascot, was visibly agitated. He paced back and forth, back and forth.

Sarah and Sophie bent to their chores, checking sales and recording the transactions in big, brown ledgers. The inventory was also painstakingly updated. CD was not a high-tech operation.

A well-dressed, middle-aged couple entered the store. They headed straight for the desks. A good sign. They meant business. "We're looking for a Herez carpet for our dining room. Old, if possible. Do you have anything to show us?"

Jon, who was already on his feet, took the challenge. A specific request was always a challenge. "We have some very interesting and unusual Herezes. For a dining room, you'll need one eight-by-ten minimum. Do you have a price range?"

"We'd like to stay under six thousand dollars. Is that possible?" the woman asked hesitantly.

"Well, let's see what there is," responded Jon. He was relieved. He had a project to keep him busy. He called Rahshi from the shipping area in back to help unroll the rugs.

There were five Persian Herez rugs in the store. As it happened, in their quest to relieve the boredom and in order to stay finely tuned, the staff at CD had recently instituted a rug-a-day review. They'd talked about the Herez two or three days before. Jon had done the research.

These people were in for a good show. Jon and Rahshi unfolded the first rug. It was a handsome rug, with a blue, green, and yellow starlike medallion on a rusty red background. The woman smiled and nodded. The man did not react. Jon went into his spiel. It was, of course, all wool, all hand-knotted, from the district of Herez (or Heriz) in the northwest corner of Persia, or Iran. Jon and Rashi opened another Herez, slightly larger and more expensive. This time the husband was enthusiastic; the wife was not happy. It was similar to the first rug except for the central medallion, which had four points instead of eight. Jon talked about the durability of the Herez because of its thick, coarse weave. The third rug was opened. It pleased no one. Jon was biding his time, saving the best for last. He and Rahshi unfolded another. It was extraordinarily beautiful and cost much more than six thousand dollars. The couple practically clapped their hands, telling each other how perfect it was for their room. No matter the money, they must have this one.

Jon advised them to take it home to try, not to make a hasty decision. They agreed and moved on to the desk area to arrange the temporary loan, peeking back again and again to admire the Herez. (Insisting that the customer try a rug at home was a successful sales stratagem.)

They left. They'd be right back with the car for the rug. Jon's dark mood was gone. There was a twinkle to his eye. An easy, smooth sell, should they buy it, which seemed likely.

"Who wants to try a tap routine with me?" Jon was currently in rehearsal for a revival of an old Broadway musical. He had the lead. He loved to dance. It was not unusual for him to break into a shuffle, soft-shoe, or quickstep every now and then.

Sarah leapt to her feet. She hated bookkeeping. Anything else, anything else. Jon demonstrated a few steps. Sarah imitated him tentatively, then again. Jon took her hand. They tried it together. Jon was singing "Once in Love with Amy" from his show, the classic *Where's Charley?* Sarah tittered. They were intent on the dance.

Sophie and Lesley looked at each other. The chemistry between the dancers was obvious. They made a handsome couple. His blond, boyish good looks were the perfect foil for Sarah's natural dark beauty: finely chiseled features, high, slanting cheekbones, green almond-shaped eyes. All that plus a long, shapely body. In the two years Sarah had worked at the store, there'd been an amazing change in her, a metamorphosis, really.

She was hired to work part-time. She had some kind of deal with Doris and Jake. Apparently Sarah had been in a blue funk, seriously depressed, and needed to get out of the house. Her three children were in school, and her buttoned-down, uptight lawyer husband, Martin Simon, was consumed with his upwardly mobile career.

The day Sarah arrived at CD she was wearing a plaid pleated skirt, a white cotton blouse with a Peter Pan collar, a Shetland cardigan, and, on her feet, flat brown penny loafers. Her gray-streaked auburn hair was cut short. She was not unattractive, just rather blah. And she avoided eye contact. But she was determined to learn the system. For weeks she followed the staff about, taking notes. On her own time, she borrowed library books and boned up on Oriental rugs.

She didn't talk much at first. Still, Sophie and Jon managed to pry some basic info from her. She came from a little town in Pennsylvania or Ohio, had attended a convent school, and had come east to attend a Catholic college near Boston. She'd met her husband, Martin Simon, at a school social, and not long after that she was firmly married and taking directions from Martin instead of the sisters. Not much there.

Four or five months into the job, the old Sarah was barely recognizable. Her hair was shoulder length and frizzed. Gone were the pleated skirts, replaced by minis or dark, slim pants. Her loose cotton blouses gave way to formfitting sweaters. She'd thrown away or burned her bras, and her figure was enviable. (The rugs were casting their spell.) One day, taking a good, long look, Jon dubbed her Sensational Sarah, and so she remained.

Sarah and Jon were buddies. Close in age, they were always huddling in corners discussing life or kidding around or playing word games. Jon prided himself in his sales pitch, and with his innate sense of style, he had much to offer. Sarah had learned from him.

The morning passed quickly. Jake arrived in a flurry with a dozen projects for the crew, but cautioned Sophie to get him out the door by 3:30. Handball today. Then it was lunchtime, the main event.

Everyone ate around the desks at CD. It was a cluttered mess, not a pretty sight. But should a customer happen in, someone was always available. (Tums were also available.) Jon unwrapped his sandwich and remarked on his wife's culinary talents. "Tuna and sauerkraut—no kidding, tuna and sauerkraut." He eyed it suspiciously, smelled it, then took a bite. He was center stage. "Not too bad." Everybody breathed a sigh of relief. Sophie pulled out a container of yogurt and a small package of raw carrots and celery sticks. She groaned and muttered but dug in. Sarah was munching happily on a giant BLT sandwich and a pile of greasy chips from the deli across the street. Lesley chatted a bit, checked her watch, and headed for the door. "Take your time," advised Sophie, "we'll cover for you." Lesley disappeared.

"Did anyone read the write-up on La Boniche today? Sounds wonderful. Three stars." A new restaurant had opened on Charles Street. Restaurants were a favorite topic at CD. Much time and thought was devoted to food. A special occasion for dining out—a birthday or an anniversary—warranted a full staff consultation. And afterward, a play-by-play, course-by-course description of the meal. Sophie took honors in sustaining interest in a memorable repast. She once spent a whole day, albeit a busy, much interrupted day, describing a gastronomic feast.

She'd been to New York to meet a brand-new grandchild (two of Sophie's three daughters lived in New York City) and while there was invited to dinner at the Gotham Grill. The meal had been superb, each course a mouthwatering delight. She remembered every detail, including the breads. She spoke in awe of the eggplant, roasted pepper, and goat cheese terrine with a basil parsley sauce, and of the arugula salad with garlic anchovy dressing. The sliced duck breast with endive and sweet potato puree was almost indescribable. She probably still had visions of the warm chocolate bread pudding bathed in a dark chocolate sauce. 'Twas an epicurean event, and she did it justice. Not only that, it hadn't made her sick. Not a twinge. (Sophie had a queasy stomach.) And the pictures of the new baby were adorable.

That particular day, lunch at the store was a washout. Nothing tasted good.

Jake had a couple more items on his project list. Jon was sent to the storage room to look for some lost saddle bags. A saddle bag made an unusual and colorful wall hanging. It consisted of two camel bags, small Oriental pile rugs, the sides of each stitched together to form an envelope, which were then woven together into one long piece to be hung over the neck of a horse or donkey and used as a carry-all. For Sarah he had a list of old but not forgotten customers. "Let's call them. Tell them our collections are better than ever and see if they're still alive." He meant that figuratively and literally. Jake was happy only when there were lots of people in his store. It happened but rarely.

A smartly attired interior decorator with a bright red cape thrown over her shoulders marched through the door. She was a great favorite at CD. "Hello, hello." She was in a hurry. She had a presentation the next day. She usually knew what she wanted. She zeroed in on the perfect rug, a Persian Saraband, just the right size. The Saraband with its rows of small *botehs* (pears) was a great favorite with the decorators. The popular paisley pattern was clearly a derivative. Its field of red and its vine borders made the Saraband a pleasant and easy rug to accessorize.

"I'll try that one. Now find me two more with similar colors. Don't strain yourselves."

She knew her clients were happy only if she gave them choices. She always took out three rugs. Two would come back, but that was okay, she was a good customer. Sophie wrote up the sales slip. The rugs would be delivered tomorrow. "By eleven a.m. Don't forget."

Lesley strolled in. She was aglow and slightly tousled. Sophie took her in hand. "Here, sit down. I'll get you some tea. Sit." Lesley grinned at Sophie. There was a whiff of booze. Sophie forgot the tea and sent Rahshi out for a large container of black coffee. "Did you have a nice lunch? What did you have?" Lesley considered the question and started to giggle. The giggles got the better of her. Sophie watched in dismay, wondering where Jake was. "He's so funny and smart." Lesley was gasping for breath. "And he's handsome, don't you think, Sophie? Isn't he gorgeous?"

"Yes, sweetie, he's very nice-looking." Oh, Lord, there was going to be trouble. Sophie had watched good old reliable Lesley, fifty years old, married with grownup kids, blossom into a lovely, amusing and probably desirable woman. Sophie wasn't sure how far Lesley was willing to chance it. It had all started right here at CD.

One day a tall, attractive, silver-haired gentleman walked into the store and headed right for the desks. "I'm looking for an old Kazak, not too big and in reasonable condition. Do you have any?"

Lesley rose to the challenge. What was so rare as a person with an appreciation for rugs, she thought. A Kazak, yet. She liked his taste. She'd researched the Kazak recently for their intramural review. It was the most popular rug of the Southern (Russian) Caucasus. Of strong reds, blues, greens, and yellows, a typical design included three aligned medallions with small interior decorative motifs. This was going to be fun.

There were only two Kazaks on hand. Lesley's customer was not impressed by either. As they spoke, Lesley learned he was a doctor and a widower. He'd recently sold his home in Cambridge and moved into an apartment in Boston. He'd given his children most of his furnishings, including his prized Kazaks. Now he was sorry. He felt the need for a few beautiful things in his new quarters, a condo overlooking the Charles River. Lesley was impressed. She promised to make a few calls to resource people. He thanked her and left. That's how they met.

Lesley and Jake conferred. Within a few days, two more old Kazaks were located and delivered to the store. Lesley called Dr. Barrett to come take a look. Again the rugs held no appeal for him. He explained that the room he had in mind required something special. Could Lesley make a house call? Although no one was enthusiastic about house calls, they did happen. Lesley got her jacket, and the good doctor whisked her away.

They must have hit it off. The house call took most of the afternoon. When a thoughtful-looking Lesley reappeared at CD, notes in hand, it was nearly closing time.

◆ ◆ ◆

Dr. Barrett's dark green Mercedes was at the curb. Lesley hopped in and off they went. To her surprise, the trip took four minutes. He lived around the corner. They parked in the garage under his building and took the elevator up to his floor-through apartment. He unlocked the door and stepped aside, allowing Lesley to enter first.

"Good heavens, what an amazing view!" She headed straight for the floor-to-ceiling window wall. The Charles River sparkled below: multiple small white sailboats bobbed in formation; across the river were the variegated stone and brick buildings of M.I.T. It was quite a sight.

"It's wonderful, isn't it?" The doctor eyed his visitor appreciatively. Tall and trim with a mop of short salt-and-pepper curls, Lesley at fifty was still a very attractive woman. In her charcoal gray suit with a jabot of creamy silk ruffles, she was the picture of understated elegance.

As he watched her, Lesley turned around. Startled by the

intensity of his look, she laughed a little self-conscious laugh and gazed about. The room she faced was wonderfully large and light with a high vaulted ceiling. Although sparsely furnished, it had a comfortable feel to it. Beige, of course. (Most men were afraid of color.) A grand piano dominated one corner. The upholstered pieces were oversized and inviting. The armside tables and lamps appeared burnished and fine. (Family heirlooms?) The polished parquet floor was bare. Just the setting for a Persian rug.

What could he be thinking? A Kazak would be wrong. Too small, too strong. Kazaks ranged in size from four feet by five feet to eight feet by four and one half feet. Nothing larger. How to tell him tactfully? Sarah was both diplomatic and kind.

"Dr. Barrett, is your heart really set on a Kazak?"

He laughed. She looked so serious. "Not for this room, it isn't. Think about what I should have in here. The Kazaks are for my study and bedroom. Somehow it's easier for me to focus on the smaller spaces. Come see the rest of my place."

He led the way. Lesley followed, marveling at the beautiful old hardwood floors and at the size of the rooms. Apartments like this were rare. The man lives well, she thought. She dug a small pad of paper out of her purse and began making notes.

"Dr. Barrett, do you know the size of your rooms, or shall I measure? I've brought a tape with me."

"We'd better measure. Here, give me one end."

He was enjoying this. How could he prolong her stay? She was so businesslike. Could he offer her a drink, some wine, tea?

"Would you like a cup of tea?" he ventured.

Lesley looked up. He was watching her again. Such a handsome man. He made her feel . . . what? Young.

"Yes, tea would be fine. Thank you."

He headed for the kitchen where she could hear him rattling dishes.

She finished her measurements, then walked through the apartment again, trying to picture the appropriate rug for each area. He found her in his study soberly considering the floor.

She is adorable, he thought. He hadn't been attracted to a woman in a very long time.

"Come, let's have tea in the living room. We'll contemplate the river."

By the time they'd finished two or three cups of Earl Grey tea, he was Peter and she was Lesley. Actually, she'd learned much more about him than he'd learned about her. She was that kind of person, warm but reticent. She kept her own counsel.

His wife had died four years ago. Badly, of cancer. They'd been married for thirty-two years. He'd given up his medical practice at that time, just closed the doors. Only research made sense. He worked now at the Mass. General Hospital, in a lab. His two sons were grown: one was a lawyer, the other a writer. Both lived in New York City. He was okay, but it was a lonely life.

He neglected to mention the women, so many women, who'd come out of the woodwork to offer him solace. They propositioned him with all kinds of inducements. He wasn't interested.

He is a very attractive human being, thought Lesley. What am I doing here? I should be getting back to work. Lesley didn't want to move. Over the years she had avoided any casual advances. Today, at this age and stage, she was drawn to Peter. How odd.

"I'd better take you back," Peter offered as if reading her mind. He was staring at her again. "Please don't be offended, but would you have lunch with me one day soon? You'd be doing a good deed, and we could discuss the rugs. Don't say no. Think about it."

Thirty years married, a good husband, two grown kids and I want to have lunch with this man. I must be crazy. What harm would it do? (Lesley too apparently suffered from Oriental rug exposure.) How provincial I am.

"I'll think about lunch," she managed.

Back at CD there was a flurry of excitement. Jackie Kennedy Onassis had just been in. (She was in Boston to attend an event at the Kennedy School of Government at Harvard.) She'd looked at an old Serapi, which she seemed to love but said was too much money. Oriental rug experts insisted that the Serapi, attributed to the town of Serab, a part of the Herez district, was in fact just a very fine example of the Herez. Sophie, Sarah, Jon, and Jake were agog. The unexpected visit had taken them by surprise. Sophie and Jake had worked with her. Pleasant and soft-spoken, Mrs. Onassis had spent thirty minutes in the store.

No one commented on Lesley's extended absence. Thank heavens for Jackie.

"How did she look? What was she wearing?" Lesley chimed right in.

Jake was fretting out loud. He should have made her a deal. Would it hurt to have Jackie Kennedy as a customer? It would be a feather . . . and Doris could get a lot of mileage out of it. He could hear her now. Maybe he could still do something. Call or write her or . . .

All in all, it had been a big day.

The afternoon at CD dragged on. Jake had run out of projects. Sophie pulled out last Sunday's *New York Times* crossword puzzle. She was addicted. Jon, sitting cross-legged on a pile of Turkish rugs, script in hand, was learning lines (for his role in the musical). Lesley and Sarah chatted quietly.

Doris called in. "What's doing?" She was talking business. Sarah gave her a brief replay. "Don't tell me they took my favorite Herez. Why did you show them that one?" There was an unpleasant whine to her voice. Sarah motioned to Jake. Let him handle this. Doris was not meant for the retail trade. Once she'd taken a fancy to a particular rug, God help the person who sold it. Doris took it as a personal affront. Although they were all aware of this little quirk, it never failed to annoy the staff person responsible for the sale.

Over the years, Doris had amassed an impressive collection of wonderful Oriental rugs of her own. It had gotten so vast that she'd had to rent storage space to contain it. She was always on the lookout for one more rare beauty. Recently Jake had put his foot down. "Not one more. We're in business to sell rugs." She had no idea that on more than one occasion he'd gone into her private cache and sold some of her beauties. She'd probably kill him if she found out. The staff had been sworn to secrecy: a little more nonsense to deal with at CD.

In private, Sophie and Lesley often discussed these extraordinary deceits. Why would Jake sell her rugs? What right did he have? They knew that they themselves were in collusion with Jake, and they didn't like the idea. What was it about? Money, probably. It always came down to money. They couldn't figure it. He didn't need the money.

They were right. He didn't need the money. It had to do with being in control. That's what it was about—control. In a marriage where one person had the money and the smarts, sooner or later the other person was bound to act out and make a stand. Jake was showing his mettle. Consciously or subconsciously, he was using his father-in-law, Meyer O. Mintz (Mom to the Mob) as his role model. Doris adored her notorious blackguard of a father. So would she feel the same way about Jake if and when she discovered his scam? (Jake was counting on her to find out.) And the profits? He rolled the money back into the business, which was to their advantage. The business had paid for them; it was a return on investment. Was that so bad?

Actually Doris had big plans for her treasured assemblage. She envisioned leaving the whole collection to a prestigious museum some time in the future. With her name on it. As a form of immortality insurance. It was important to her. The Seagulls had no children.

It was 3:30. Jake packed his briefcase. Time for handball. He was out the door. Within seconds he was back with another thought for the day. He left again. Two minutes later he was back with an idea for a new window display. Then he was gone. It never failed. They called it his yo-yo farewell.

The phone rang. This time it was for Jon. It was Nedra, his wife. Jon listened awhile. His brow furrowed. He bit his lip.

"I told you I'm not interested. Forget it. You don't listen. I'm sorry if you're upset, but that's how I feel. We'll talk again tonight. It's busy here. I have to get off." He hung up and strode to the back of the store, where he resumed pacing.

Unfortunately, the private lives of the staff people were hardly private. The telephone situation being what it was, each one knew more about the others than he or she should. A closely knit group, they had been bonded even tighter by this confidential information.

The women eyed one another. Sophie gave an exasperated sigh. Lesley nodded. Sarah got up and went to Jon.

"Can this marriage be saved?" Lesley asked Sophie for the umpteenth time.

"Not the way it's going. One of them has to bend. Both, actually. They need professional guidance. There are so many issues."

The two women sat silently reflecting on Jon's plight, or what they knew of it.

Jon grew up in New York City. He wasn't exactly an only child. There was a brother, but he was seventeen years older. Though his parents were loving and caring, they were old to have a youngster around. They left Jon pretty much on his own.

He heard a lot about his brother, but he rarely saw him. When Jon was a baby, brother Carl was in college. He was a good student and a great athlete. When Jon was a teenager, Carl was making his mark in the world of finance. A boy wonder. By the time Jon was in college, Carl was a wealthy man, married with three children of his own, living the good life in Fairfield, Connecticut. Apparently he didn't share his good fortune (in dollars and cents) with his folks.

Jon came to Boston to attend Tufts University. His parents had enough money set aside to pay for his college degree.

Jon had a head for the arts, not business. Nor was he an athlete. Still, he maintained that his four years of college were the best years of his life.

He joined Tufts' drama society, Pen, Paint, and Pretzels. Soon he was appearing regularly in every school production. He became a familiar figure on campus. And he loved his art classes. That's where he met Nedra.

Nedra O'Hearn was his professor of art history. At the time, she was a newly appointed assistant professor. It had taken her years to achieve that title. She was a serious artist as well as a historian. Passionately devoted to her field of expertise, she'd had little time to spare until she met Jon.

With her long, dark straight hair, loose ethnic robes, and dramatic pale makeup, Nedra looked the part she'd been dealt. A father who'd deserted his wife and baby, a mother in vaudeville who'd abandoned her only child. Fortunately, there was a loving grandmother struggling to make a home for Nedra, who, not surprisingly, was a very serious child and an excellent student. She worked her way through college and was halfway through graduate school when fate intervened once again.

She'd been studying late at the library. Not watching the clock, she was taken aback when the lights blinked on and off, on and off, which signaled closing time. She hadn't intended to stay so late. The last bus was pulling out as she hurried to the stop. Damn! She stood there a minute or two, wondering what to do. In the distance she saw a group of kids heading her way. She felt uneasy and turned looking for a lighted store or some other people. Nothing. Panicked, she started to run. She could hear loud, strident voices, and then the group of kids, in reality a street gang of angry delinquents, was in hot pursuit. They caught her, gang-raped her, beat her senseless, and left her for dead. A patrol car making its rounds spotted a body on the sidewalk. On closer inspection, the officer saw signs of life and radioed for an ambulance.

She was in the hospital for eight months. They'd patched her together, then done plastic surgery to camouflage the scars. Fourteen operations in all. The mental anguish was not as easy to treat. No amount of therapy could restore Nedra's soul, the trusting, fragile inner spirit ravaged that awful night.

Still, she got up off the ground and went about living her life. Several years passed. Then Nedra met Jon—beautiful, gentle, nonthreatening Jon. There'd been no men in her life since her shocking attack. The thought of anyone invading her body disgusted her. Now she felt the kindling of long-suppressed desire.

Fifteen years older than Jon, she was oh-so vulnerable. As he courted her, first with apples for the teacher, then with tiny bouquets of exquisite flowers, she began to thaw, then warm and finally blossom. His youthful enthusiasm coupled with his sensitivity and charm won her heart.

Their unlikely romance was the talk of the school. They didn't care; they were in love. The day after his graduation, they were married. He moved into her apartment.

There were problems from the start. Jon needed a job. His brand-new liberal arts degree got him nowhere. He would have loved a job in an art gallery or an antique shop, but that didn't happen. Nedra's friends were condescending towards him. Faculty events were difficult. In private, they were love-birds, in reality, the going was tough.

Being young and full of zest and in love, Jon pooh-poohed Nedra's fears. He was the optimist. Not to worry, he'd find a job. They should be thinking about a baby, that's what they should be doing. Nedra was working hard. As the wage earner, she faced a pile of bills each month. She'd love a baby with Jon, but what then? He said they should be looking for a house with a big backyard. How? With her terrible history, she'd never allowed herself such high hopes.

Jon prevailed.

He got a job in sales at a fancy haberdashery, Louis of Boston. It wasn't what he wanted, but for the time being, the pay was okay. They bought a decrepit old house in Reading, and were in the endless process of transforming it into a wonderfully eclectic Victorian abode. And Nedra was pregnant. Those were the good times.

The baby was born. Heidi, they called her. She was a delight. Nedra felt well and strong. Jon adored his little family.

Nedra had to go back to work. Money was the problem, as usual. The house sucked up every dollar they earned. Jon was looking for a better job. An intriguing want ad in the *Boston Globe* caught his eye: *A person to sell Persian carpets.* He loved beautiful Orientals. He'd grown up with old Sarouks. He remembered the rosy pink Sarouks with their all-over floral spray designs. (At least his mother thought they were Sarouks.) He'd be terrific selling Orientals. He answered the ad, and that's how he came to CD, full of promise and with a keen interest in the merchandise.

Right away he loved everything about Classic Design. It was fun, and it was easy, and so he stayed too long. There was time for amateur theatrics (he joined a drama group in Reading), and time for Heidi, and time to putter around the house. He was comfortable and happy, though he knew he had dead-ended. (Jake was a great believer in permanent status quo.) Jon wasn't a hustler, and that was making Nedra crazy.

She was doing double duty. She was ambitious and worried. Twice she'd been passed over for promotion. No matter, she was writing a history of the Flemish masters. If she ever finished it, the book would do wonders for her career. Jon was the problem. He brought home so little money, and he demanded so much attention. She tried to spend as much time as she could with Heidi. He didn't seem to understand. He was still a little boy himself. She was feeling frazzled.

The latest blow-up was about insurance. Not health insurance for a change, but life insurance. Someone at Tufts had advised Nedra that life insurance was essential. Considering her age and background, she didn't need much convincing. Jon thought the idea ridiculous. His career had yet to take off, and they couldn't afford it. Nedra was insistent. Their viewpoints were askew and they were both very stubborn.

Pigheaded was more like it. And that was their problem of the day.

At CD Sophie had gone out to do her errands. Lesley was sitting at the desk, thinking of Peter. He is a love. Sweet, considerate, and fun. He's added another dimension to my life. (They'd had lunch together several times.) Am I going to bed with him? I don't know. He says it's my call. One day I can't wait; the next, I'm appalled at the thought. What's the matter with me? Ken and I are devoted to each other, have been for thirty-some years. I try to be a good wife and mother and, damn it, I am! Still, Peter makes me feel like a kid. I'm practically in heat when I'm with him. Hope it doesn't show. What about the silk lingerie I've been buying? For years I've worn plain cotton bras and panties. Ken won't notice. Then it must be for Peter. Okay, I'm wavering. More than that. I've taken to shaving my legs twice a week. I'm on the verge. A happily married woman who's never strayed, never had an affair, I'm about to fill in the blanks. Big, fat deal. It's ridiculous. I'm ridiculous. Here's a customer. Enough. "May I be of any help?"

Plopped on a heap of Chinese Orientals, Jon and Sarah had been talking, seriously, it seemed. They were expounding on their problems. Or rather, on Jon's problems. Sarah was a good listener, and Jon needed someone to hear him. He went on and on. Sarah was concerned; it showed on her face. Jon stopped suddenly. "Let's have a drink at the Lenox before we catch our buses. Okay?" Sarah nodded.

Sophie was back at her desk, straightening the messy pile of papers, pictures, letters—the accumulation of a day's work. The phone rang. Someone was looking for Jake. Not easy. "Try tomorrow between twelve and three." Lesley and Sophie divvied up the closing chores and it was 5:30 P.M. Day was done. Exit the troops.

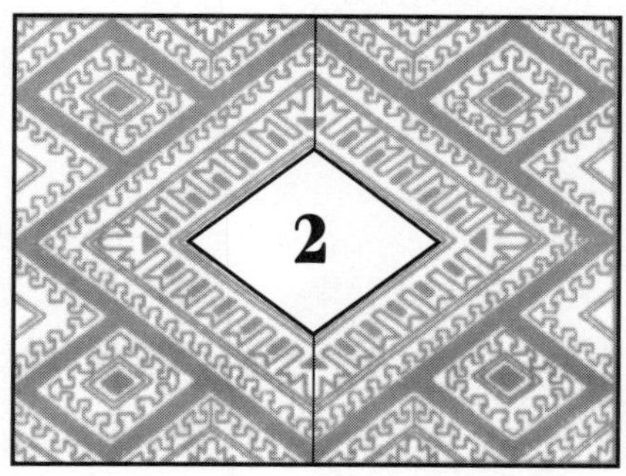

The next morning an emergency dentist appointment made Lesley late for work. She and the mail arrived simultaneously. As usual, Sophie sorted it, sniffed out the important stuff, and slit open the envelopes with payments enclosed. She opened a small, square vellum envelope and pulled out an elegantly engraved card. It looked like an invitation. She read it, gasped, and burst into tears, handing the card to Lesley. Lesley stared at the formal announcement. Tears welled up in her eyes and coursed down her cheeks. Billy! Darling Billy! Dead at thirty-two. A tragedy, a terrible waste.

All that day and for weeks after, Sophie and Lesley reminisced about Billy Barnes. Although his escapades at CD were legendary, only Sophie, Lesley, and the Seagulls had been witness to them. Many moons ago, Billy had added a measure of festivity to the store. That was the only way to describe it.

Jake and Doris had found him working as a waiter in a trendy new restaurant in Cambridge. (The Seagulls ate out more often than not. They loved finding new places that they frequented continually until they discovered another, better new place.) During their patronage of Tapas, they got to know Billy pretty well, or so they thought. He was endearing and anxious to please. He'd made a big impression. (Having no children of their own, the Seagulls were, perhaps, more gullible than most.) They must have mulled it over at home, pro and con. Who knew? Anyway, contrary to their own very strict policy, they invited Billy, with no references at all, to come to work at Classic Design.

He was out of Tapas like a shot. Lesley and Sophie didn't know what to make of their new co-worker at first. He was tall and slight with a shock of wavy black hair. He had an impish, infectious grin and a twinkle to his eye. He didn't know a thing about rugs, but he was a born salesman. And charming. Not particularly interested in the merchandise, he could wing it, making up stories about each item, with the best of them. With Billy, hard sell made its first appearance at CD. Over coffee and during lunch, the women got to know a great deal about Billy, much more than Jake and Doris ever dreamed.

He was gay, unashamedly gay. An overnight case was stashed in the coat closet with his jammies and things should he want to sleep over with some new friend. (The rug magic probably exacerbated his condition.) He was from the South and proud of it, with a slow, honeyed drawl. How he'd come to Boston was another story he hadn't shared with the Seagulls. Marooned seemed to be his present state.

He'd been living and working in Atlanta. One night after work, he'd stopped for a drink at the Westin Hotel, where there happened to be a big biotech conference in progress. The place was jumping. A good-looking stud, obviously from the conference, had come on to him, loud and clear. They'd spent the night together. And the next. And the next. By the time the convention was over, Billy was in love. So was the bearded man, who turned out to be a professor at Harvard University. They made plans for Billy to come north.

Billy wasted no time. Within days, he'd bagged his affairs in Atlanta, had flown to Boston, and was happily ensconced in the professor's townhouse in Cambridge. According to

Billy, they had two wonderful years. Billy loved Boston and its environs. He was a peacock. His lover plied him with gifts of clothing and jewelry. He loved strutting his stuff, and he was a fun companion. He cooked and took care of their home. They frolicked together in the oversized hot tub, scrubbing and playing with each other while sipping wonderful rare wines, according to Billy. Then the professor lost interest. Just like that. No warning. Billy was heartbroken. But being young and fairly pragmatic, he moved out and moved on.

His first job as a single person in Boston was at Tapas. His second was at Classic Design.

The pace at CD quickened. Billy was more interested in clothes than either Sophie or Lesley were. With his incessant nagging, the two women began to spruce up for work. His nod of approval in the morning gave them a charge. Labels impressed him. He'd pull back the neckline of their blouse, sweater, or jacket to see if he recognized it. They didn't like that. He made them a little crazy.

He spent all of his time and money on clothes. He was adorable. His wardrobe was ultra-fashionable. Before the outfits were advertised in *GQ* or *Esquire,* they could be seen in Boston (never exactly known for high fashion) on the one and only Billy Barnes at CD. He knew instinctively what was in.

Jake didn't always relate to Billy's costumes. One day, in the heat of summer, he took exception to a new see-through, raggedy cotton jersey that Billy was wearing. He sent him home to change. Sophie and Lesley nearly fainted as Jake read Billy the riot act. But with a big grin and a wink at the women, he was off. No problem.

More often than not, his clothes were wonderful. He'd heard about a Ralph Lauren outlet store in Lawrence. He'd rented a car to get there. From that little expedition, he'd gone into big debt. A long black double-breasted, beaver-collared overcoat was the piece de resistance—it was gorgeous on him. There was an assortment of soft, hand-woven Italian sweaters, not to mention shirts, slacks, and a beautiful pair of suede boots. He was the best dressed person at CD, no contest. Jake looked positively shabby next to him.

Billy spoke often of his kid sister Sally. He doted on her. She was a "hoot," he said. When she finally came to Boston, no one knew what to expect. Typically, and going deeper into debt, he'd hired a dove gray Mercedes limo complete with chauffeur for the entire weekend of her visit.

She looked just like him, had all his mannerisms and the same slow drawl. She was still a kid, tall and gangly, but verging on real beauty. She was enchanting. They told each other everything, all their secrets. He took her to the best restaurants and to see Bette Midler, who was appearing in Boston that weekend. They had a great time.

Sophie and Lesley learned a little more about Billy's family. His father was a retired military officer. His mother, a free spirit, was an interior designer. She also ran a kitchen-and-bath shop in Charleston, South Carolina. They were very close. They talked on the phone daily. He also had an older brother whom he never saw. Bare bones stuff.

During the two years Billy worked at CD, the public was becoming more and more aware of AIDS. The press was getting the message across. The reports were ominous. No one wanted to talk to Billy about AIDS. If he brought up the subject, okay. He went for a blood test and said it came out fine. He said he guessed he'd never make forty, that he'd settle for a short, sweet, happy life. Sophie and Lesley felt sad and uncomfortable when he spoke like that.

Still, most of the time, he made them laugh. When Lesley was doing groundwork on an apartment hunt for one of her daughters, Billy came to the rescue, translating the current real estate jargon, junior grade. A "smoking crib," according to Billy, was a great find, a hot apartment, requiring a quick decision.

Then Billy got wanderlust. His love life needed a geographical boost. Two weeks notice, and away he went.

He seemed to find happiness back in Atlanta, working as a decorator in a furniture store. Oft-times he'd call or send a postcard to "whom it may concern" at CD. He kept in touch. One postcard said he was going home to Charleston for a while, he wasn't feeling right. His mom was going to fix him up.

Sophie and Lesley were suspicious, but neither one wanted to talk about it. A few months later, they each received a long, sad letter from Billy recounting his days at CD and reminding them what fun it had been. He had personal messages for both of them. He was wrapping up loose ends, no doubt about it. The women were heartsick. They knew he was saying goodbye in his letters, but the formal, engraved announcement still came as a shock.

"Sophie, this has his touch. I bet he chose the card and wrote the inscription." Elegant and gallant. Brave and foolish. That was Billy Barnes.

Ever since receiving the sad news, Sophie and Lesley had worn the small red satin ribbon commemorating those who had died of AIDS. Each day, without fail, they pinned the bright symbol to their blouse or jacket. They would not forget Billy.

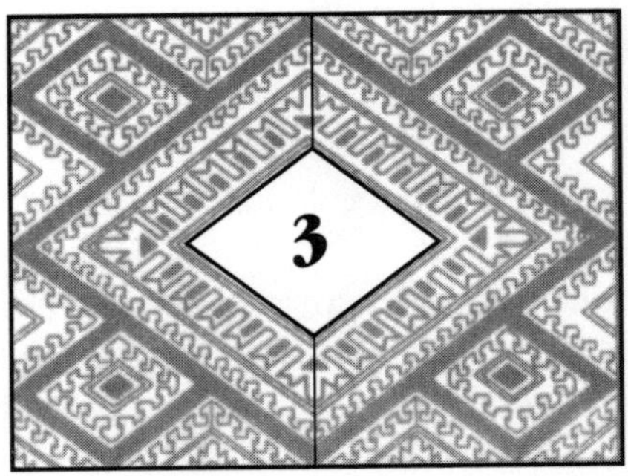

A few weeks later at CD, Sophie was dealing with a client at the back of the store. Jon and Sarah were busy with inventory. Lesley sat alone at the desk. Lost in thought, she smiled inadvertently. She was remembering her big scene. It had just happened three days ago on her day off.

She'd had lunch with Peter at the Ritz. They'd had chicken salad with capers and polished off a bottle of Pouilly-Fumé. A harpist played softly in the background while they talked and talked. It was very lovely. Then in a warm, rosy glow, she'd gone back to his apartment and climbed straightway into his bed. Peter tarried discreetly in his study. She'd taken off all her clothes, folded them neatly in a pile, and gotten under the covers, tucking the quilt up under her chin. That it was almost like a visit to the doctor's flashed through her mind. She giggled nervously. Peter was a doctor.

He came into the room. He was wearing a white terry cloth robe. Naked underneath, she assumed. First he closed the window blinds—very thoughtful. Then he shrugged off his robe and slid into the bed with her. It happened so fast that Lesley hardly glimpsed his body. He reached for her; she turned to him. They kissed slowly, deeply, wetly. His hands began to stroke her bare flesh, cup her breasts. Wow! As he explored her every part, she heard, "Lovely, beautiful, fantastic." What a turn on! Lesley was gasping as she began her own search-and-stroke mission.

He was broad of shoulder and flat of stomach. His nipples grew erect as she fondled them. Her hands moved slowly down over his belly, his groin, down. Being simultaneously petted and handled herself, she was practically aflame when her hand lightly touched upon his penis. Her fingers gently manipulated his sac, then his shaft, but instead of growing bigger and harder, it began to shrivel and go slack. Good heavens! Was she doing something wrong?

"Peter, are you okay?" He mumbled something, reached for his robe, and was out of bed before she knew what was happening. Still gasping, she heard the water running in the john, the toilet flushing. What?

Peter returned to the bed, shamefaced and quiet. He explained to her that he hadn't been with a woman for a very long time, and that he guessed he couldn't perform anymore. He was embarrassed and sorry. Could she forgive him?

Quick to size up most situations, Lesley had been thrown for a loop. Gathering her wits about her, she snuggled next to Peter, making soothing noises and all the while assessing the problem. He needed a little help, that was all. Besides, she would not allow her first affair to fizzle before it began. Good old reliable Lesley to the rescue.

"Peter, do you find me desirable?"

"You know I do."

"No man has ever moved me to such passion as you just did."

"What good was it? Nothing happened."

"Peter, do you trust me? Then lie still and let me do for you."

Forevermore when Lesley reviewed the secret pages of her life, she would think with wonder and amazement of that first afternoon with Peter when she not only revived his sagging libido, but transformed him into a raging bull. She was sore for days after.

Lesley kissed him sweetly as if he were a little boy, then searchingly till he responded. She kissed his face, his ears, his neck, then mounted him and, straddling him, her ample breasts grazing his skin, she kissed and nuzzled and licked the entire length of his body. As her fingertips lightly encircled his male organ, kneading it and playing it like a musical instrument, his sex grew large and hot. He was groaning; she was moaning. Still her thighs gripped him in a vise. With a start, he broke away, turned her rapidly over on her back, and thrust into her, lusty and sure. In a galloping frenzy they rode to an astounding mutual climax, much to their wonder. They were both panting as he rolled off her and lay by her side.

After a few minutes, Peter took her left hand in his and kissed it. Several more minutes passed. Her hand was still in his. Then propped up on one elbow, Peter spoke softly, "My gypsy woman of witchcraft and magic, how would you like to do that again?" Lesley's eyes flew open. He was serious. They were too old for this. She was just regaining her equilibrium. Well, why not?

"This time, my lovely, you lie back and I will pleasure you." She did and he was true to his word. His long tapered fingers worked over her whole body, her breasts, her sex, dipping into her wetness, massaging her clitoris. She was almost mad with desire before he entered her, slowly, leisurely. Lesley abandoned herself to a yellow world of steamy, erotic sensuality. Unabashedly, unrestrainedly, as one their bodies blended into a throbbing, undulating wave of pure physical euphoria. Surging, cresting, climaxing, they moved together, then coasted breathlessly back to consciousness.

They lay side by side, exhausted but luxuriating in an exquisite sense of well-being. Lesley arched, stretched, and reached for the quilt. Peter laughed at her sudden reticence and threw the coverlet to the floor. He was enjoying their nakedness. He hadn't a clue to Lesley's psyche. How could he? At that moment, she really needed to cover up. He, by the same token, really needed to cuddle and fondle her. Post coitus, it was his nature.

But he'd underestimated Lesley. As he ran his hands over her full, soft body, tickling her breasts, caressing her mons, she became aroused again. She looked at him with alarm. "Shush, it's all right. Relax." Cradling her upper body with one arm, his mouth on hers, his fingers slipped into her very moist vagina. Sighing deeply, Lesley gave herself to the moment. His insistent, wet, internal probing made her tremble. She couldn't help herself. With a small cry, she exploded into her third orgasm of the afternoon. When she could speak, she whispered primly, "That was very nice. Thank you," and fell fast asleep. Peter covered her carefully and tenderly with the quilt.

When she awoke, he was sitting in the armchair by the window, watching her, a big smile on his face. He was fully clothed.

"Peter, darling, don't look at me like that. I'm a mess. What time is it?"

"You, my sex goddess, are a sight to behold. You're glowing. How old did you say you were? And what are you doing in my bed?"

"Don't tease me. I'm a fifty-year-old woman badly in need of a nice hot shower. Just point me in the right direction."

When she had showered, dressed, and put on some makeup, she felt marvelous. She found him in the study. The sight of her calm and collected, clad in a smart glen plaid suit and black silk shirt, pearl buttons at her ears, the red AIDS ribbon pinned to her lapel as usual, unnerved him. He felt like undressing her.

"Lesley, we've got to talk."

"I'm starving. I've got to eat something or I'll faint. And there's nothing to talk about."

"How about some cheese and crackers? Some wine?"

"Fine. Make sure I'm out of here in half an hour. Ken said he'd call early tonight." (Husband Ken was in Chicago on business.)

"I can't let you go before we sort things out."

"Peter, don't be silly. What is there to sort out? We're about to have an affair, that's all. I'm not a sex maniac. Something happened today. You happened. Why can't we be grateful that we're so compatible physically?"

"Lesley, you're not that worldly wise. That much I know. Today was extraordinary. You were extraordinary. We'll have our affair, but it's not going to be that simple. You'll see." With that he took her in his arms.

Coming to with a start, Lesley, looking slightly dazed, opened the ledger and started to sort accumulated invoices. She'd think things through another time. There was plenty of bookkeeping to keep her busy today. Fortunately.

The day had started well. An important architect had stopped by to choose rugs for a client. Whereas a decorator arrived with fabric samples and paint chips to coordinate with floor coverings and agonized over exact shades and sizes, an architect dealt in concepts: color, space, line. He made quick decisions. Jon and Sarah, working together, had organized an entire houseful of handsome old Persians. They'd had a good time. At the moment the rugs were out on approval. There was no way of knowing if they were in fact sold, but the chances were excellent. If so, the tab would be astronomical. Everybody was in good humor.

When Jon and Sarah decided to take their sandwiches outside and find a sunny spot to lunch, Jake, in a jovial mood, had told them not to hurry. "Take your time," he'd said.

They'd been meeting after work at the Lenox bar once or twice a week for a couple of months. They'd shared some pretty intimate stuff. Both thirty-two years old, securely married and with children, they'd admitted that life seemed to be passing them by on a few basic pleasures. Sex, for instance. It was not what they'd hoped or assumed it would be.

In Sarah's case, Martin insisted upon a regular routine: sexual relations twice a week, allowing fifteen minutes per encounter, start to finish. No experimenting, no deviating, no excitement. For Martin, sex was another discipline in maintaining good health. Sarah, with her strict religious upbringing, halfheartedly agreed.

Nedra, Jon's wife, was another story. She was a reluctant sex partner. At first, eager to please her young husband, she'd faked enthusiasm. With her history, it was understandable. Jon, a careful, patient lover, eventually aroused her real interest if not great passion. She seemed to enjoy the basic act, but any slight variation and she froze. That's how it was. Jon understood. Still he was healthy and able-bodied, and he yearned for more. Lately Nedra was usually too tired for any sex.

Once Sarah and Jon understood they were in the same boat, they began to look at each other in a different light. Wondering. Could they? Should they? (Without a doubt, they were overexposed to the rugs.) What about their mates? Big question. Could two people have a physical relationship and just remain friends? Neither one was sure. But they were mightily tempted.

There was another issue involved, though unspoken. Sarah and Jon were well aware of the AIDS epidemic. Didn't Sophie and Lesley wear their red ribbons every day? No way would they put themselves or their mates at risk. They were monogamous. Sarah had never slept with anyone but Martin, and she was positive that Martin didn't fool around. Jon admitted to a couple of youthful peccadilloes, but that was before Nedra, and Nedra was afraid of men. Besides, they'd both been married ten years. No, they didn't have to worry about AIDS. Other matters, yes.

They walked over to the parklike mall that bisected Commonwealth Avenue, found an empty bench, and sat down to stare at the four-story red brick building at number 190. Chewing solemnly on their sandwiches without much appetite, they contemplated the scene. Jon had an old college buddy from Tufts who lived at number 190, and who had offered him, with a wink and a leer, his not-so-humble abode for daytime assignations.

"It's ours if we want it, Sarah. All I have to do is make arrangements for the keys. Shall I?"

Unwilling to make the decision, Sarah took another tack.

"Let's get a sex manual first. As a guide. How about *The Joy of Sex*? I've heard it's pretty good. We'll divvy the cost. But let's find a store where they don't know us. It's embarrassing. I feel like a teenager," she laughed.

Jon tried again. "I'll get the keys. Okay? We'll buy the book and read it together over there." He pointed to 190 Commonwealth.

Sarah nodded. They finished lunch, stuffed the leavings into a trash barrel, and hurried off, hand in hand, in search of an anonymous bookstore.

When they got back to CD, Jon was carrying a plain-brown-paper-wrapped package. They were both giggling.

"What's so funny?" said Jake "How about sharing the joke? We could use a little fun."

With that, Sarah and Jon looked at each other and cracked up. Sarah tried to speak, but it was no use. She was convulsed.

Jake, Lesley, and Sophie couldn't help smiling, watching the two now shaking with laughter. It was infectious.

"When and if you comedians recover, see me. I have some work for you. Then I'm leaving. Handball today."

The phone rang. Lesley picked up, Sophie went back to the bookkeeping, and Jake headed for the back of the store, looking for his briefcase.

A few moments later, Lesley put down the receiver and turned to Sophie. "That's odd. Another rug theft. One of our best customers, too. Someone else called last week about an insurance claim on a rug purchased here. Also stolen. Good thing we keep records. 'Course, most of our things are one of a kind. But there's always the next best thing. Oh well, I suppose this is good for business."

"What a thing to say," from Sophie.

Lesley and Sophie often kidded about the benefits of divorce to the store. Once a couple became accustomed to living with beautiful carpets, they were hooked. Should the marriage break up, the carpets became pawns in the divorce settlement. The loser, more likely than not, returned to CD to find replacements. It happened time and time again. The same thing would hold true for thefts. The rugs were gone. They had to be replaced.

"Think about it, Sophie. If someone takes your rugs, you still need rugs. If your insurance covers it, you're all set. You can have the fun of choosing again. I admit, not everybody thinks that's fun, but some will. It's not our fault, and we still stand to benefit. Jake will love it, you'll see."

As it happened, Jake was in a hurry. Big match. There was no time for discussion. The day dragged on.

Sarah and Jon, sitting cross-legged on a pile of Chinese rugs, were perusing *The Joy of Sex*. Sarah's face was crimson. She was looking at the illustrations. She was not happy. Jon was wide-eyed and beaming.

"This is going to be great. I think I'll buy some K-Y jelly." He looked at Sarah and stopped smiling. "What?"

"I don't know if I can go through with this. The pictures frighten me. I don't want to be tied up."

Jon laughed. "Sarah, we're playing. Who said anything about bondage? We'll do only what we both want."

Jon had much too much experience with an inhibited woman. He didn't need another. Perhaps they should reconsider.

"Let's really think about this. We'll bury the book under the Chinese pile here and play it by ear. Look, it's five o'clock."

Another day drew to a close at Classic Design.

◆ ◆ ◆

Lunchtime the following week. Jon and Sarah were standing at the door of apartment 3D, 190 Commonwealth Avenue, grinning at each other. Jon fumbled with the key and opened the door. He bowed to his companion, then walked in ahead of her.

"Anyone home?" he called. Silence. "Come on in, Sarah. The coast is clear. Welcome to our secret garden."

It was a smallish three-room apartment, surprisingly neat for a bachelor's pad. White walls, black leather sofa and club chairs, chrome-and-glass occasional tables. The walls were hung with colorful framed posters. There was a big, white fluffy Flokati rug covering a good part of the hardwood floor. Sarah and Jon chuckled when they saw it. It was a standing joke at CD that single guys always fell for flokatis. There was something very sexy about the handwoven Greek rugs. Maybe it was the long, shaggy, natural raw wool. The tiny bedroom boasted a king-sized bed with a bold black-and-white plaid spread. It took up the whole room. Best of all, the ceiling was mirrored.

Jon and Sarah shucked their jackets and plopped down on the whooshy leather sofa. Sarah was clutching *The Joy of Sex,* now in a plain white paper cover. Jon emptied a small plastic bag, out of which rolled a tube of K-Y jelly and two packages of condoms.

"We seem to have everything we need," said Sarah. She had definitely resolved her ambivalence. "I think we'd better start from square one. You show me yours, I'll show you mine," she laughed. She started unbuttoning her blouse.

"Wait, let me do that. I'll undress you, you undress me," said Jon, striving to match Sarah's mood.

What started as a good-natured game progressed to a heavy-breathing striptease. When they were both naked, they stood looking at each other in awe. His broad shoulders and full chest tapered down to a narrow waist and slim hips. His legs were long and well muscled. The hair on his chest and pubes was blond and curly. As he gazed at Sarah, his male organ swelled and swayed.

"God, you're well hung," murmured Sarah without a trace of shyness.

"Look at you, Sarah. You're absolutely magnificent. I'm speechless. I had no idea."

Sarah was almost as tall as Jon. Her breasts were full and firm, her waist narrow, her hips curved, her stomach flat. She was a beautiful woman in her prime. She didn't flinch from his admiring gaze.

"Let's do some touching and feeling and see what happens. We have to get back."

Trying to keep it light and easy, Jon threw his arms around her, intending a big bear hug. But as their naked bodies made contact, an electric current charged through the two playmates, leaving Sarah visibly shaken, and Jon gasping for air. He nudged her into the bedroom, where they collapsed on the bed. Unable to speak, they began touching and feeling one another; their safety precautions lay neglected on the coffee table in the next room. But not forgotten. As they continued exploring each other's nooks and crannies, they came dangerously close to the cutting edge, where passion consumed conscious thought.

"Whoa," yelled Sarah. Jon stopped short.

"You've got to be kidding," he panted. "This is not good for my health."

"Too bad. I think we'd better finish ourselves. You know, masturbate. Here's some Kleenex. I'll watch you; you watch me."

"Where do you get your ideas, Sarah?"

But Jon required no coaxing. His member was large and hot, and with just the slightest rhythmic pressure, he blew his cork. He lay, momentarily spent, at Sarah's side. She was fascinated. She lay back, and handling her own immediate needs, she was soon shuddering and quivering alongside Jon, who was astonished by her performance. They were still for a few minutes.

Then a startled "What time is it? We've got to get back. Quick, get dressed. Hurry. Jake will have a bird."

In no time flat they were fully clothed, the apartment ship-shape, their equipment was retrieved, and they were out the door.

Their sheepish return to CD went unnoticed. Jake was not around, and both Sophie and Lesley were busy with clients.

So began their genial and rewarding sexual alliance.

The next week. Sophie and Lesley were working meticulously at the monthly billing. The two women, veterans of the task, chatted as they stacked the bills alphabetically. The phone rang. Lesley picked up. Cradling the receiver with her shoulder, she continued writing the statements.

"Classic Design," she said crisply. "Yes, Mrs. Hutchins, I'll tell Mr. Seagull you'd like to speak with him. Is there anything I can do in the meantime? He won't be in until tomorrow. You sound upset." She listened for several moments, then spoke.

"No, not all of your rugs! Even the Bakhtiari! I can't believe it. When did it happen? Did they take anything else? What a shame! I'll pull your file. Now, don't worry. I'll check the original invoices and get replacement estimates. Mr. Seagull will call you first thing in the morning."

Sophie stopped what she was doing. A puzzled expression flickered across her face. She waited for Lesley to put down the phone.

"What's going on? That's the third customer in two weeks to report rugs stolen. Our rugs."

The phone again. Sophie answered. She listened intently, motioning to Lesley.

"I'm so sorry to hear that, Mrs. Potter. I know how much you loved that rug. Yes, it was a very rare and unusual Tabriz. Maybe the police will find it. You can't tell. Of course I'll get the information for you. Mr. Seagull will be shocked. I'll have him call you tomorrow. He's out of town today. Goodbye."

The two women looked at each other. Lesley spoke first. "Four robberies, rug robberies, in two weeks. All happening to our clients. Very strange! Jake had better do some calling around. I wonder if any other store is getting these calls? Shall we try Gregorian's?" Gregorian's was the leading Oriental rug dealer in the area. "Maybe not. We don't want to start any rumors. Can it be a coincidence?"

Sophie, biting her lip and frowning, was lost in thought. She was startled by Lesley's question.

"A coincidence? Not likely. But let's take this a step further. If only *our* rugs are being stolen, then somehow we're involved. Not directly, but in some way. How? Crooks aren't selective. Real pros might be. It's not easy to steal a rug. Think about it! We need more facts. I'm calling Jake."

Jake was unavailable.

Sophie wisely cautioned Lesley, "Let's keep this to ourselves. No point getting everybody excited."

So it was another ordinary day at CD. Sarah sent out an old Chinese rug, circa 1930. Prices were low then, $225 to $375 for a nine-by-twelve foot rug. This particular Chinese rug, in reasonable condition, now costs $4,500. Lesley sold a small Persian Afshar, a handsome tribal rug. The colors were strong, reds and blues, with a diamond-shaped medallion on a field of stylized flowers. The Englishwoman who bought it was anxious to learn all about the rug. Lesley told her what she knew: that it was made by nomads living in the area between Shiraz and Kirman in southern Iran; that the basic size was five by six feet; that there was always a little white or cream in the pattern; and that it was all wool and hand-knotted. Two or three more people wandered through, and that was that.

The next morning the phone was shrilling as the crew trekked into the store. It was not Jake. It was another customer reporting a stolen rug and looking for particulars on current values and availability. It was clear now, to Sophie and Lesley anyway, that a major problem was developing. If other dealers were involved, it was a headache but manageable. If CD had been singled out and only its customers were being targeted, then it was going to be a mess.

When Jake ambled in at eleven, Sophie, the designated informant, took him to the back of the store and quietly brought him up to date. In her usual competent manner, she outlined the problem. He looked serious by the time the impact of the situation hit him. He went back to the desk and made three or four seemingly casual calls to other rug stores. Nothing was amiss. Now he looked worried and grim.

"Jake, these are the people who phoned. I told them you'd get back as soon as possible." Lesley handed him the list.

"I don't want to make the calls here. There's no privacy. No sense broadcasting the problem. I'm going home. Doris is at tennis. Call me if anything else happens." He was out the door.

"That was quick," noted Sophie. In the eighteen years that Sophie had worked at CD, she'd never seen Jake so upset. And with good reason. What next, she wondered.

"The police are bound to show up," said Lesley. "I think we'd better tell Sarah and Jon before that happens. They've gotten awfully chummy lately. Have you noticed? They're practically inseparable."

Sophie had noticed. It had something to do with the rugs. She'd known for a long time. Some mysterious something about the rugs. They'd all been affected. She too. A few years ago, an elegant older gentleman, a legend in local music circles and a good customer, had insisted she come to tea at his home. And she had gone. Not once but five times. She was pleased and flattered by his attention. it could have easily become a habit, and Lord knows what else. The man was really charming. But the thought of her three adorable grandchildren and her dear old solid-as-a-rock husband put the kibosh on a budding relationship. Just in time. It was a struggle to stay away from Leon. If she'd been of a younger generation, it might have been a different story. She was still sorry. So damned straitlaced. It was how she'd been brought up.

A confidential powwow was held at the desk. Jon and Sarah were told of the stolen rugs. Excitement at CD was so rare that it took a few minutes for the facts to sink in. They were asked not to talk about the thefts.

"It's a mystery, and we're all part of it," insisted Jon.

"Why do you say that?" asked Sarah.

"If all the stolen rugs come from here, then it has to be an inside job. Somebody here is connected to the robberies. Anybody can figure that out. But who? And why?" asked Jon.

"Let's think about this, and then we'll schedule a meeting with Jake. Maybe we can dredge up a clue or two," suggested Sophie. She had to agree with Jon about its being an inside job.

"What about the guys in back? They actually handle the rugs. They pack them and ship them, sometimes they even deliver and lay them. They know where to find our rugs. That's something to keep in mind," commented Sarah.

"It's mind-boggling if we have to consider all the men and boys who've hauled rugs for us over the years. There have been dozens, maybe more," added Lesley.

Jake called in. He spoke to Sophie for several minutes. She remained poker-faced. When she put down the receiver, she said, "It's worse than we thought. There have been eight house break-ins reported. Fifteen rugs stolen. All of them ours. How do you figure that? A crack police detective has been assigned the case. Meanwhile, all rug dealers in the area have been alerted to be on the lookout for hot merchandise. So far Jake has been able to keep CD's name out of the papers. Publicity would kill us. Who would even want a rug from here, given the possibilities? What a rotten shame!"

Nobody had much more to add. The discussion petered

out. They went back to their chores quietly, each one of them trying to remember anything that could be relevant.

At home, Jake, in shirtsleeves, was going through some old files in his basement. He was trying to work up a list of all the stolen rugs, not only replacement information for his clients but a master list for his own use. The thieves knew what they were doing. Only the finest Persians had been taken. Taken where? Should he be warning his customers with valuable Orientals to be on guard? No. Should he tell Doris what had happened?

At that moment, he heard the back door slam and footsteps overhead. Doris was home, back from tennis. She called his name. "Jake, are you home? Are you okay? Why aren't you at work? Is it the car? I told you something was wrong. Where are you?"

"I'm down here in the basement, hon. I'm fine. The car's fine. But there is a little problem. I'll be right up." He took a deep breath, gathered his papers together, and headed up the stairs. He never knew what to expect from Doris. Sometimes she went berserk over nothing. Other times she was the rock of Gibraltar. He'd learned to tread carefully.

She was standing by the sink gulping down a glass of cold water, still in her white tennis togs. Explaining cautiously about the stolen rugs, all of them from their store, he was surprised and relieved to see her reaction. She smiled. To her it was funny? Not appropriate, given the ramifications, Jake thought. She didn't understand.

"We'll sell them all more rugs. It's a boon for us. Why do you look so unhappy?" asked Doris.

"If this gets out, we're finished! The publicity will put us out of business. Only the rugs that *we've* sold to these people have been stolen. Only *our* customers! I don't know what's going on, but I tell you, this is real trouble."

"Don't be so dramatic. A few rugs are stolen. So what? It happens. Life goes on."

Jake said nothing. He'd lived with this woman for thirty-five years. He knew about her constant struggle with anxiety and stress, the endless therapy. He'd shielded her from many a nasty situation. Now, in an undeniable crunch, she was cool as a cucumber. She didn't get it. That was all he could figure. This indifference to trouble was a switcheroo. Jake knew how Doris depended on him for constant reassurance, that he was her security blanket. It had been so, right from the beginning.

"I'm taking your clothes to the cleaners, and then I'll do some marketing. Is there anything special you'd like for dinner?"

Jake stared after Doris as she walked out of the room. He'd been begging her to take his clothes to the cleaners for days. As for dinner, they'd been eating out every single night. Doris hadn't felt like cooking. Now this. He hoped she was okay. He had enough to worry about.

At the store Sophie, at Jake's request, was trying to put together another list: the men and boys who'd pulled and lugged rugs over the years. Not an easy task, considering the employee files were in Jake's cellar. A few she remembered vividly.

Pedro, for instance, who was a sturdy, Buddha-like figure of a man. She could picture him now perched squarely on his favorite pile of Orientals. He'd worked for years, silent and obliging and strong as an ox. He could lift anything. He'd be here yet if his son hadn't squealed on him. Luis had come in one day while Pedro was out to lunch and asked to see Jake. After a brief conversation, he had left. Jake wandered about the store mumbling to himself for some time. It seemed that the wonderful Pedro was withholding vital information. He wasn't sixty-six as he claimed; he was actually seventy-eight years old. And lifting heavy rugs! After that no one had the heart to let him pull rugs. So against his will, he was retired with a big party and all the trimmings.

No, Pedro was not involved.

How about Rahshi? He drove a big pink Cadillac, a better car than his boss. He was always talking about the clubs he frequented, and last year he'd made a trip to Mecca. He didn't make that much money.

Okay, Rahshi was a possibility.

Loshi and Lensin, the young Tibetan men, were too gentle and kind to be suspect. They lived with their brother in Cambridge. He was a monk, for God's sake.

Forget Loshi and Lensin.

There was Paulo. Everybody loved Paulo, but his long-distance romance with Tonya was troublesome. He was planning a trip to Russia this year. Where was he getting the money? Such a romantic! He'd met a girl at an airport, a girl accompanied by her mother, spent seven hours with her (and her mother), and fallen in love. (It was the rugs. It had to be.) Paulo hadn't been the same since. He called Tonya once a week if not more. He'd shown everybody at CD a dainty gold-and-diamond wedding band he'd bought for her. He kept it wrapped in a bit of tissue paper in his wallet. How did he manage?

Sophie hated to think it, but yes, Paulo had some explaining to do.

Tim. A smart-aleck kid heading for big trouble. A Southie who thought gang rumbles were fun. Sophie hadn't recovered from his last gang encounter. He'd shown up at the store the morning after with a huge bandage around his neck. His throat had been slashed. "Eighty stitches," he'd announced proudly.

"Didn't that hurt?" Sophie had asked.

"I didn't feel a thing in all the excitement. A rumble is a real high," was the answer.

No, not Tim. He wasn't smart enough.

She'd almost vouch for Phil and Gus and Juan, the current rug pullers, but what did she know? Clearly this was a case for police professionals.

Sarah and Jon were atwitter over the robberies. Since their initial encounter at 190 Comm Avenue, they had both been hyper, Jon more so than Sarah. Just thinking about the gourmet sex menu now readily available had him rushing to the men's room to jerk off. It was happening so frequently that Jake was concerned. He'd given him the name of a good urologist. It was laughable.

Sarah was sympathetic. She was similarly afflicted but okay during the day. At night, lying next to the somnolent Martin, not so. Her sexual fantasies ran rampant. Too bad Martin was such a prig! He was missing out. Oh, well. She tucked two fingers into her vagina, and slowly and carefully, so as not to disturb her husband, she massaged her tensions away.

At the store, when they weren't discussing the robberies, they were planning their next rendezvous. "Lunchtime Wednesday. Let's hope we can get away. In the meantime, we'll draw up a plan, every which way we ever thought of doing it."

"Don't laugh. I'd like to try it standing up," said Sarah. "And I've been thinking that as long as we have no illusions about what we're doing, the language is important. We're fucking, okay? Screwing, maybe. Not balling. Too macho."

As Sarah went on, Jon's prick took heed and sent him rushing to the men's room. Again. When he returned, he begged Sarah to confine herself to the written list. They were itemizing different ways of fucking, and in what order they were going to try them. (They were sitting on a pile of Persian rugs, which would account for their rutting obsession.)

A customer walked into the store. The entire staff was so preoccupied with lists that the woman had to ask for assistance, unusual at CD. She was looking for a large Kirman, a rather formal Persian rug. It was not a favorite with anyone at Classic Design, nor were there any examples on hand. There was, however, a picture card file showing available Kirmans. Named after the city in Southern Iran, where they had been made since the sixteenth century, they were of rather elaborate floral design. In America, a thick pile rug with a central medallion on an open cream, beige, or white ground was standard Kirman fare.

Lesley, who had been consulting with Sophie vis-a-vis lists, deftly handled the Kirman request. The staff was so accustomed to and immersed in tribal rugs that the flowery, more elaborate Orientals were often given short shrift. She tried to explain the virtues of a Tabriz or even a Tibetan, but the woman was adamant. She had her heart set on a Kirman. "Pictures don't help me," she announced disagreeably. Sensing a no-win situation, Lesley apologized and suggested that the woman try Gregorian's in Wellesley. She wrote down the address and phone number and handed it to the flabbergasted customer.

Watching the woman march out of the store, Lesley reflected upon why she found tribal rugs so appealing. The primary colors and the bold designs struck some basic inner chord. She responded to their primitiveness. They're getting to me, she thought. No, they've gotten to me. Lesley had always considered herself a levelheaded person. Not lately. Case in point: her unlikely behavior with Peter. Think of something else! Stolen rugs. Right!

But the more Lesley mulled over the matter, the more peculiar it seemed. The rugs were valuable—that was a given. Not easy to translate into cash. Why steal rugs? Why not silver or jewelry? Did thieves specialize? It took time to steal a rug. How did they do it? With a truck parked out front? Too crazy. It didn't make sense. Every time she thought of it, she came to the same conclusion.

She'd missed the point. Not Sophie, who was sitting at the desk contemplating the same matter. Jon was right. It had to be an inside job. She was studying the individual card files of the victims. Each card was a dated, descriptive record of their rug transactions. What was she looking for? Some connection. They'd all been good customers for years. So what? Sophie had an odd feeling that she couldn't explain. There had to be a connection. She stared at the files spread out in front of her, gave an exasperated sigh, shuffled them back into a neat pile, and reached for the bookkeeping ledger.

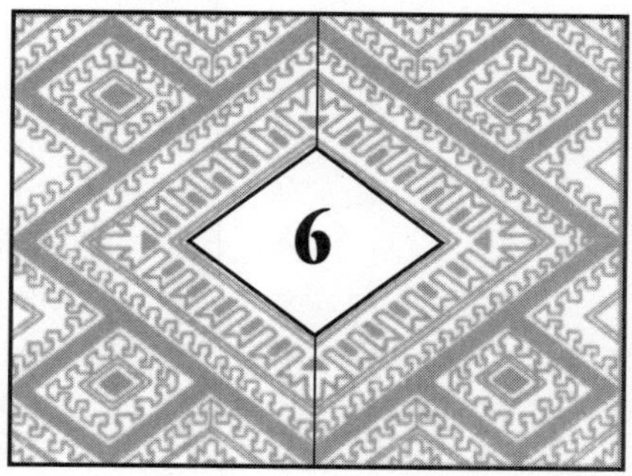

Detective Lieutenant Mike Hannagan, Precinct Four, Boston Police Department, was in for some serious razzing. He was sitting calmly at his desk, reading from a big book propped up in front of him, and he was taking notes. The book, *Oriental Rugs and the Stories They Tell,* by Arthur Gregorian, was an oversized volume with a multicolored picture of an exotic rug on the cover. From time to time, he reached for the coffee mug on his desk and took a swig.

Hannagan didn't kid around. He was handed the rug case; he didn't ask for it. If he had to become a goddamned expert on Oriental rugs, so be it. Breaking and entering was a crime, a felony. Enforcing the law was his job. He figured out how and why crimes were committed and apprehended the criminals. The district attorney's office did the rest. For breaking and entering the sentences were stiff: ten years daytime; twenty years after dark; lifetime if carrying a weapon.

A graduate of the School of Criminal Justice at Northeastern University, Hannagan had been a plainclothesman for the last twelve years. Although his was a cerebral approach, he'd won grudging respect and approval for his success in the field.

Still, he took a lot of bullshit. His colleagues were giving him the business today.

"What do you have there, Mike? Aladdin and his frigging flying carpets? Is that how they got away? They flew?"

"That's a possibility," he nodded good-naturedly.

At the moment, he didn't have a clue. He'd checked out every one of the rug heists. He'd gone over the scenes of the crimes. He'd interviewed the victims. Nothing! Well, not exactly nothing. He knew he was dealing with pros. The thefts were slick, clean as could be. The Mob? Naw! They wouldn't bother with such stuff. What about the little rug store on Boylston Street? He'd investigated the list of employees and former employees, and other than a couple of immigration violations, there wasn't a suspect in sight—at least not on paper. I've got to go rug shopping, he vowed to himself. It's time to meet the folk at Classic Design.

His first foray on CD took place the following Saturday. It was a bright sunny day and the joint was jumping. The door was wide open and people were strolling in and out. Sightseers, maybe. Hannagan was surprised by the crowd of people in the store. He joined the throng, but instead of moving right along, he lingered.

The floor was awash with carpets in an extraordinary variety of jewellike tones: corals, blues, greens, golds, crimsons. Mike excused himself repeatedly as he stepped gingerly over the rugs. He counted six salespersons busy with customers. He was surprised by all the activity. Saturday was a big day. From his paperwork he thought he could identify the six: that had to be Jon Hedstrom; she was Sophie Weiss, for sure; that was probably Lesley Kane; the gorgeous broad was Sarah Simon, stacked in spades. I've met Jake Seagull at the station. He didn't recognize me. So the gray-haired old bag must be his wife Doris. They said she was the rug maven. That's the cast up front.

Mike looked at the merchandise with keen interest. Until

now, Oriental rugs were not his bag, not within his experience. You had to get used to them, he thought. They were an acquired taste. I bet that's a Bakhtiari. Looks just like the one in the book. It was easily recognizable with its all-over squares, each one containing a stylized flower. The rich dark-blue background was typical, so too the green, red, gold, and yellow of the design. Yes, Bakhtiari! And there's a Bokhara! No mistaking the velvety red rug with its orderly full-field rows of octagonal guls, often described as elephant feet. He turned over the tag on the Bakhtiari and broke into a sweat. Ten thousand bucks! That's why cops didn't know from Orientals. He ambled about, playing a little game, seeing if he could name the rug.

He was so preoccupied with testing his new knowledge that Sarah startled him a bit with her "May I be of any help?"

"I'm afraid I can't afford anything in the store," he replied truthfully.

Sarah regarded the tall, stern, rugged man dressed in jeans and a tweed jacket and knew intuitively that he would be important to her. What she actually said was, "We have a layaway plan for people who love rugs but can't afford to buy them all at once."

"I'm afraid even that won't help." He meant, Be forewarned, lady; I have no money. Hannagan was also having an intuitive flash. What's Sarah Simon doing in my future? She's a married woman. Her husband's a lawyer yet. I don't want any trouble. Hannagan had been married and divorced. He knew trouble.

He said, "Don't bother with me. I'm just enjoying the rugs."

Hailed by another shopper, Sarah was quickly caught up in the challenge of finding the perfect rug for someone's large, sunny dining room. "No reds, please." Not easy.

Then, without any fanfare, in strolled Fritz Weiner, accompanied by one of his young assistants. Weiner, the week's distinguished guest conductor of the Boston Symphony Orchestra, was in Boston for a series of four concerts. Due to constant media coverage, he was a familiar figure, one of the few superstars in the field of classical music. It was his first time at Classic Design. Jake and Doris had the grace to be in awe as they asked his pleasure. He wanted a small, quiet Oriental for his study in his home in Switzerland. He was pleasant but very particular. Only one rug, a lovely old Melas, interested him. It was a prayer rug from Anatolia in soft, warm colors ranging from gold to brick red. The niche was rust-colored, topped by a pale area with stylized floral elements. No, he didn't want to try it. He'd think about it. Please to give him the information. Doris obliged, and he was gone. Just like that.

Mike, along with a dozen other fascinated browsers, watched the brief transaction. It was a different world. He spent ten more minutes admiring rugs and observing the scene and the staff. He wasn't sure why, but he was getting the message that the action was here. And his hunches, crazy as they might seem, usually paid off.

Monday morning, bright and early, Hannagan strode into CD again and officially introduced himself. The staff greeted him enthusiastically. Sophie and Lesley had been expecting him for days. Jon was eager to be of help. Sarah, blushing as she recalled their encounter on Saturday, was excited about the investigation. They offered him coffee, which he readily accepted. Then, parked on the end of one desk, styrofoam cup in hand, Mike Hannagan was put through the third degree by his own group of possible suspects.

"How were they stolen?"

"Were there any witnesses?"

"Have you recovered any of the rugs?"

"Are there any other stores involved?"

"Why rugs from CD?"

"What's the motive?"

"Good, tough, logical questions. Very impressive. Do I have any answers for you? Not yet. What I'd like to do is talk to each of you individually. There may be something you know but maybe you think it's not important. Anything that comes to mind regarding the case, anything at all, no matter how wacky. Before we start, I want to get my bearings. Tell me about these file cabinets. What's in them? Are they locked? Who has access?"

When he heard that the cabinets were never locked and were fair game for whoever might be interested in their contents, he was not pleased. He asked Sophie to jot down a brief description of the files for him.

As it happened, Sophie, Lesley, and Jake were constantly at the files. The bookkeeping required it. Sarah sometimes, and Jon almost never. Bookkeeping was not a part of his job.

"What about Mrs. Seagull?" inquired Mike.

"She does just about whatever she wants to do here, but she's rarely at the files. No, that's not entirely true. Last month she spent some time checking the records of former clients. She—the Seagulls are planning a big mailing promotion," responded Sophie.

"Is it possible for someone else to get into the files unobserved?" asked Mike.

There was some discussion on this point. Lesley and Sophie insisted that it would be impossible. Sarah and Jon weren't so sure. When they were all busy with customers, who was watching the files? On a busy Saturday, for instance. They couldn't agree. Farfetched, the detective concluded.

Mike needed more coffee. He hated his caffeine dependency, but it came with the territory. There was a Coffee Connection down the street. Saying he'd be back in twenty minutes, he left abruptly.

"Now we're getting somewhere. This guy knows the score. He looks like a younger version of Clint Eastwood, don't you think?" suggested Jon.

"I wouldn't like to meet him in a dark alley, if that's what you mean," said Lesley, "but I feel better knowing he's on our side."

Sophie had a funny feeling—call it a premonition she shared with no one—that the outcome of this bizarre situation was going to be grim. "Yes, I agree. If anyone can, Mike Hannagan will get to the bottom of this."

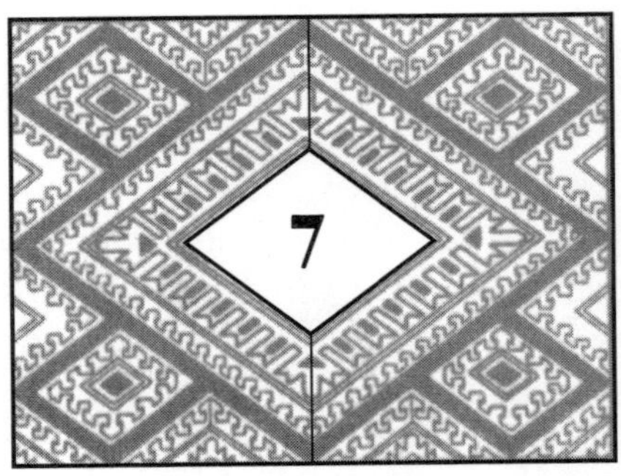


It was a beautiful, sunny day in the neighborhood. Sarah and Jon were hurrying over to their trysting place on Commonwealth Ave. Trysting place was not an apt description of their secret lair; playground or gymnasium was more like it.

As they unlocked the door and entered the welcoming apartment, Sarah dug into her capacious leather shoulder bag and produced the list. It was tattered and stained. They'd had many a discussion and many a cup of coffee over the list, but no action. Today was the day.

They headed for the bedroom with its huge bed and mirrored ceiling. Sarah pulled her tight black sweater up and over her head, revealing her beautiful bare breasts. No bra.

"Sarah, how is it possible for a mother of three to have firm, stand-up boobs?" Jon cupped her breasts, then leaned over to suck a nipple. She moved away to strip off her skirt, slip, and pantyhose. When she was completely naked, she turned to Jon, who was struggling to contain himself. She helped him out of his clothes. He motioned her to the bed, but she shook her head no.

"Standing up, remember?" she reminded him.

The position involved some thoughtful calisthenics. With six-foot Jon backed up against a wall, Sarah, who was five foot ten herself, embraced him, raising her right leg and swinging it over Jon's left arm for support. Her sex was now accessible. A little fumbling, some manual help, and there was penetration.

"Don't you dare go off until we get the feel of this," cautioned Sarah. "I think I like it. How about you?"

"It's great, but I'm getting a cramp. I can't tell where. God, that feels good."

They wiggled and gyrated, enjoying the new sensations. As the motion intensified and Jon began to pump in earnest, Sarah, standing on one leg, was thrown off balance. They started to fall still firmly engaged at the groin. In midair, they came apart. With a crash they landed in a heap on the floor. They lay there, stunned. Then:

"Are you okay?" from Sarah.

"I guess so. Are you? Did you come?" asked Jon.

At that, they burst out laughing. The laughter escalated into shrieks of hilarity. They were literally rolling on the floor.

"Jon, could you get me some ice from the fridge?" gasped Sarah as her laughing fit subsided.

"What do you have in mind now?" asked Jon suspiciously. "We're running out of time."

"I hit my arm on something. I can feel it turning black and blue. Ice will help."

Naked as a newborn babe, he was off and running. Moments later he was back with a bundle of ice wrapped in a dish towel. Sarah applied it to her sore arm. They sat together on the floor, companionably close.

"Let's forget standing up; it's too hazardous. I'm glad we tried, though. Aren't you?" asked Sarah.

"I suppose so. Sarah, listen, if you could have anything you wanted, what would it be?"

Sarah thought about Jon's question and frowned. She was not an introspective person. She admitted she didn't know.

When she posed the same question to Jon, he had a ready reply.

"I'd be out of Classic Design in a minute. An antique shop of my own—that's what I'd like. I'd be good at it too, but it takes money. That's my dream. Oh, well," he sighed.

As he rubbed up against Sarah, his shaft grew hard again. They came together in the old missionary position without a word of protest on her part, and finished off their lunch hour in a blaze of mutual pleasure.

The one thing missing in their rendezvous was food. No time. They were both starving when they got back to work. They had to send out for two hearty, stick-to-the-ribs corned beef sandwiches.

At home that evening, after the children were in bed, Sarah and Martin were watching television together. That meant Martin, as usual, had the remote. It was his choice and he was watching the ball game. Sarah was daydreaming.

"Martin," she mused, "if you could have anything you wanted, what would it be?"

"Shh, I'm watching the game."

Sarah got up and went into the kitchen.

Later that night, as they were getting ready for bed, Martin said, "About what you asked before. I have everything I want so far. A prospering law firm, a family, this house, and great expectations. What else is there?"

He yawned, got into bed, and snapped off his bedside lamp. In three minutes he was sound asleep.

There must be something wrong with me, thought Sarah. He's got it all, and he's a pompous ass. Reflected glory is not my style. So what *is* my style? Damned if I know. I love my kids, but they're growing up. They don't want me hovering over them. Why do I feel like I'm on hold, waiting for something to happen? Sarah got into bed, picked up *Gourmet* magazine from her bedside table, and was soon lost in a travel article about the beautiful old towns along the Tyrrhenian seacoast south of Naples, Italy.

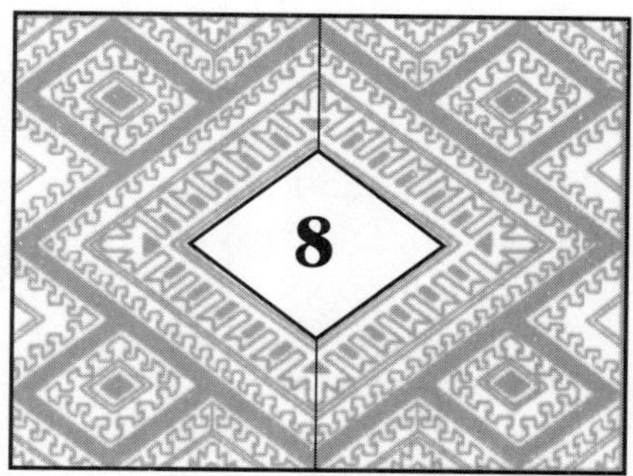

At their corner table in the Ritz dining room, Lesley and Peter were lingering over coffee. Even though they frequented several restaurants in the neighborhood, the Ritz was their special place. So far they'd been lucky; no unwelcome chance encounters. Usually, at this point, they were in a rush to get back to Peter's apartment. Not today. Why was he dawdling? Lesley wondered. When he asked her to share a dessert, a piece of cheesecake, she knew that something was up.

"Not cheesecake, Peter, that's more sinful than adultery," she replied glibly. She thoroughly enjoyed every moment with this man, but the clock was ticking, and their time together was limited. "Have the fresh raspberries and blueberries. That's good for both of us."

Lesley was into health foods, had been for years. She was concerned with diet and exercise and was earnestly trying to convert Peter to her way of thinking. Cheesecake, indeed! She realized Peter was stalling for time. But why?

At that instant, Peter pulled out a small silver package tied up with a blue silk ribbon. "Lesley darling, I have a gift for you. Don't be upset. When I saw this at Shreve's, it looked like you, exactly right. I knew. Please, I want you to have it."

Shreve, Crump and Low was a Boston landmark. Founded in 1796, it was the premier retail firm in the area dealing in fine jewelry, silver, china, and antiques.

Lesley was surprised. And speechless. He handed her the present, which she unwrapped carefully, revealing a longish gray velvet jewelry box. Her eyes were misty even before she opened the little case. When she did, she gasped at the beautiful, glowing string of pearls nestled into the black satin cushion. She burst into tears.

"I love them. They're wonderful, but you mustn't. It's too much. I can't accept such an extravagant gift."

Lesley had coveted pearls like these most of her adult life. She knew much more than she should about her gift. A rope of pearls this quality, eight millimeters at least, perfectly matched, opera-length ran into thousands of dollars. If she ever knew that Peter had in fact paid $8,000 for her pearls, she'd go to pieces.

"Lesley, you've brought joy back to my life. Put them on. Please, darling, put them on. They're made for you."

She dabbed at her eyes with her handkerchief, then took the pearls from the case. As she slipped them over her head, settling them smooth as silk against her neck, she had an overwhelming desire to wrap this man in her arms and never let him go. So much for affairs! Under the circumstances, with the whole world watching, she said urgently, "Forget dessert. I need you now. If we hurry, we can be back at your place in ten minutes."

"Not today, my sweet one. I have another little surprise for you." Peter signaled the waiter for the check.

A few minutes later, they were alone in the elevator going up. "Peter, for heaven's sake, get this car going in the right direction. I think I'm in heat." He laughed delightedly and swept her into a big hug.

"Hold on, woman, we're almost there." The elevator jerked to a stop. Peter pushed Lesley out on the twelfth floor and led her down a plushly carpeted hallway to room 1232. Pulling a key card from his pocket, he unlocked the door and bowed to Lesley. She grinned at him and waltzed into the bedchamber, which was abloom in soft rose, peach, pink, and green flowered chintz. Blossoms on the chairs, on the windows, on the coverlet. A king-sized floral canopied bed sat imposingly to one side.

It's perfect, she thought. He is the dearest man. I'm in love with him. Damn! This wasn't supposed to happen.

Unzipping, unbuttoning, and shedding her clothes as she moved, except for the gleaming pearls, she was up and onto the inviting bed in no time. Peter was right behind her.

"Lesley, today is special. Lie still."

He kissed her eyes, her cheeks, her nose, her lips. His insistent tongue found hers. Her body writhed. She felt damp between her legs.

"Don't bounce, darling. Try to stay still."

With that he mounted her and eased into her wetness, moving up, up into the core of her being. They were united. Quietly they lay together. Very soon, Lesley felt a primal stirring deep within her. She tried not to move as the stirring gained momentum, but she was overcome by wave after wave of pure physical euphoria crashing over her, carrying her beyond anything she had ever experienced. Peter was swept along in the rushing tide into a flood of sensual pleasure. Time stopped. Surge and retreat. Surge and retreat. Again and again. Slowly, quickly, slowly.

As the storm subsided, Lesley, holding on to Peter for dear life, sobbed into his neck.

"Lesley, my dear one, that was an act of love. Fine and true. I love you. I want you. You must stop crying and speak to me."

"Peter, what happened? What was that? Tell me."

"According to the textbook, if I'm not mistaken, that was a vaginal orgasm. You, my dearest, are one of the lucky few, very few, who've ever achieved such a thing. I knew it! I knew you could. I knew it! Of course, you have me to thank," he laughed.

"Peter, I love you, I do. I never thought I'd say it. If you ask me, I'll stay in this room with you forever. But if we have to deal with real life, I don't know. Be careful of my pearls," she added with a little sniffle.

He laughed again as he rolled to her side. He slipped one arm under her shoulder, and in that position, with the flowery quilt resting lightly atop them, they fell asleep.

It was dusk when Lesley opened her eyes. She stretched and moved closer to Peter. He was wide awake and ready for her.

"Peter, thank you for every minute of this wonderful day. And the pearls. I shall wear them and treasure them for as long as I live. I have to get home. How can I leave you?"

He held her in a loose embrace, their bodies barely touching. He spoke.

"Lesley, I'm serious. I need you. Every time we make love, and afterwards you run home to Wellesley to Ken, how do you think I feel? I'm angry and lonely. I want you to live with me, to spend the rest of your life with me. I want us to be married."

"Darling, please. I'm already married. Ken and I have been together since college. We have two kids, a lot of history. I can't explain it, but I still love him. I love you both. Is that possible? Don't look so hurt. I'm in over my head. You were right the first time. I'm not that sophisticated."

Peter had a sinking sensation that Lesley meant what she said. Still he had no intention of giving her up. Lately he'd felt the need for a permanent relationship. It was a good feeling. It was about rejoining the human race. He knew he had Lesley to thank.

"Come, let's shower. There's a great big bathroom to chase you around." Peter pulled her out of bed. "About today, my darling, you were primed and ready to go off without one bit of foreplay. That's because most of the foreplay took place in the dining room."

"You never touched me."

"Ah, but I did. The one thing, the only thing that sex therapists agree on is that the brain is the primary erogenous zone. It all starts in the head. That's how I got to you, my adorable one. You were ripe for the plucking. You're lucky. Sex is easy for you, and you enjoy it so. You look prim and proper. No one would ever dream you harbor such a voluptuous, carnal appetite."

"Now I'm blushing. I'm not like that at all, not a bit. It's you, Peter. I just look at you and I want to make love to you. It's you. At this stage of my life, it's a miracle. I feel young again. I can't bear to leave you, but I do. Then I count the hours till we're together again. In between I live a semi-normal life with my dear, comfortable husband in suburbia. It doesn't make sense."

"You worry me, Lesley. What if Ken finds out? Then what?"

"I couldn't bear it."

"That's . . . irrational."

"I know."

When they were showered and dressed and ready to leave, Lesley reminded Peter to be extra careful about security in his building. "Make sure you turn on your alarm system when you go out. And tell your doorman to beware of anyone carrying rugs, no matter the reason."

The staff at CD had agreed not to talk about the stolen rugs. Lesley was concerned about Peter's newly acquired Kazaks. She'd sworn him to secrecy. She trusted him implicitly.

One last embrace, and they were out the door.

"Next Wednesday—I'll call you at the store."

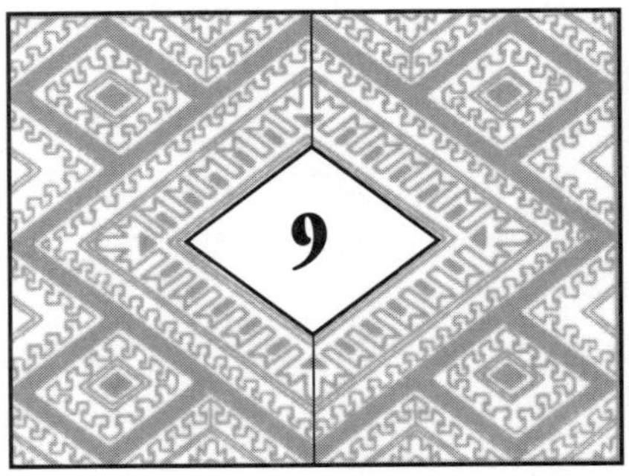


Mike Hannagan was fast becoming a fixture at Classic Design. Every day he dropped in for an indeterminate length of time. If the staff were busy, he entertained himself looking at the rugs. He was getting good at identifying them, which was no small accomplishment. So far he could tell a Bokhara, a Joshaghan, a Saraband, a Meshkin, and possibly even a Tabriz. There were so many variations of the Tabriz that it was confusing. Hunting designs, vase designs, and the ever-popular center medallions. Who could tell? The main colors were supposed to be blue, ivory, and orangy red. So how come the soft pastels? No, Mike didn't have a handle on the Tabriz yet. Wait. He did know the difference between a kilim and a knotted rug. That was easy, piece of cake. The kilim was flat-woven, reversible, and had no pile, the knotted rug had both heft and pile. Not too shabby for a Mick from Southie, he thought.

Other times he kibitzed with Sophie or Lesley or whomever happened to be at the desks. As casual as it might seem, Hannagan was working, trying to fit the pieces together to solve his case.

Trained to observe, he'd picked up some odd behavior.

Mrs. Seagull, for instance. She was the star of the show; she knew her stuff. But she was a bundle of nerves. When she was in the shop, the tension was unmistakable, almost palpable. The staff stepped carefully. It was evident that she resented his presence and his camaraderie with the help. She wanted him out. Still, when he'd questioned her, she remembered more details about each rug than anyone else in the store. Besides that, she had a genuine fondness for the merchandise. So why was she reluctant to talk about the robberies? And how come she seemed so unconcerned?

Maybe worth a little background check.

Like everyone else, Hannagan had lost his heart to Sophie. She'd worked with him on the files, patiently explaining the whys and wherefores. She knew everything. She was caring and helpful and very hip. Her quick sense of humor had smoothed over his awkwardness in unfamiliar territory. She was one nifty broad. He owed her.

Lesley Kane was not an easy read. She was pleasant and cooperative and apparently a pro in her field, but something was on her mind. He wagered it wasn't rug thefts.

Look into.

Jon Hedstrom was a nice guy, maybe a shade too dapper for Mike's taste, but so what? Jake and Doris treated Jon like dirt. Mike wondered why he took it. He didn't know from rug heists. Looked like he and Sarah had something going. Lucky bastard!

Sarah Simon. She was friendly and standoffish both. He knew too much about her. Nothing to do with rug heists. She was a coffee fanatic. He kept bumping into her at Coffee Connection. Sometimes she'd sit with him over hot java, sometimes not. Always in a hurry. She was a secret lottery player. He'd followed her and watched her buy her ticket at the lottery sales place. She spent two dollars a week—no more, no less. She was really serious. Poor baby, it was a sucker's game.

Okay, he'd become obsessed with Sarah Simon. That face, that body. He wondered if she knew. He'd seen her watching him. I must be losing it, he decided. It's this place. I get a hard-on every time I walk through the door. God Almighty!

Hannagan did his homework. He'd turned up some interesting matter. Lesley Kane's affair with Dr. Peter Barrett probably accounted for her being so preoccupied. Too bad. Nice people shouldn't fool around. Too much at stake. And they didn't know when to quit.

He'd uncovered the love nest at 190 Commonwealth Avenue where his gorgeous Sarah was cavorting with Jon Hedstrom. Damn it to hell!

But the big surprise of the investigation to date was Mrs. Seagull! Mrs. Seagull, Doris, the tweedy dried-up Brahmin lookalike, was in reality the only child of the notorious Meyer O. Mintz, paternally known to the Mob as Mom. At one time he'd run the numbers racket in the Northeast. He'd been a constant thorn in the side of the Boston Police Department. They'd managed to nail him two or three times, but each time his smart-ass lawyers had gotten him off. He'd served a few months for tax evasion, nothing else. That was long ago. Mom had been dead nigh onto twelve years. Left a pile of dough too. So he brought up his little girl like a fairy princess, sent her off to Wellesley College for polishing, and lo and behold, a well-bred, blue-blooded, cultured lady. Doris Mintz Seagull. Revisionist history. How did she remember Daddy? Fondly, he'd bet.

Hannagan had a bunch of pieces, none of which fit together. He was getting an in-depth feeling for his unlikely suspects, but there was something missing, something important. What? Back to Classic Design.

These days he was greeted warmly. Even Jake Seagull was getting used to him. "Anything new turn up?" asked Jake. Seagull was worried, had been all along. Way to go.

"We're working on it," said Mike. Hannagan didn't blame Jake for the muttering under his breath. The case was taking far too long. He decided on another tack.

"I'd like to talk to you and Mrs. Seagull away from the store—at your home, if you don't mind. Some morning this week. You name it."

Jake was surprised but agreeable.

"Thursday is okay, I think. Let me call Doris. She's the busy one. How about ten a.m. Do you know where we live?"

Mike assured him that he did, and that ten o'clock Thursday was fine. He wrote it down on a piece of scrap paper. Now he needed coffee. Where was Sarah? She understood the coffee hang-up. They had that in common.

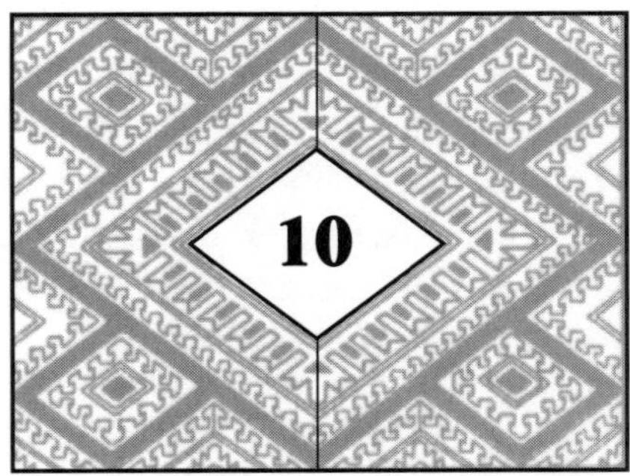

For years the staff at CD had wondered about Jake's morning tardiness. He said he was working at home. Doing what? There had even been snide remarks about the possible sexual proclivities of the Seagulls, remarks that met with either smirks or groans depending on the person's imagination.

Truth was the Seagulls did indulge themselves in the mornings, and they liked it kinky, the kinkier the better. Doris was a firm believer in sex toys and had accumulated more than a few. Their toy box included a number of porno films, vibrators of every size and shape for him and for her, penis enhancers, and even a sport sheet or two. Most of the stuff came out of catalogs.

It wasn't always so. In the beginning their sex life was very traditional. Jake was happy enough and thought Doris was too. He was no sexual athlete, but he did his part. No one complained. Then, one morning out of the blue, he woke up to a strange humming and the sight of Doris grinding her hips right by his side on their king-sized bed. It took him a minute or two before he realized what she was doing. She was playing with a vibrating gizmo and she had it stuck up her *yoni*.

"What're you doing?" he croaked in his raspy, early-morning voice.

Without missing a beat, she panted, "Quiet, I'm coming."

And in a flurry of sheets and blankets, she came. Jake was practically thrown off the bed in the upheaval. He couldn't help noticing it was a much bigger climax than usual.

"What's the matter with you? Where did you get that thing?" He was hurt. That was his first reaction. He wasn't enough for her. His macho self-image had just been wounded.

"Relax, I bought one for you too," cooed Doris in a very laid-back voice. "It's great. Wait 'til you try it."

"Doris, are you crazy? You could electrocute yourself. I'm not trying anything," he snapped.

Right away he was sorry he used the word *crazy*. Goddamn it! She was so vulnerable. The struggle to maintain her cool was never ending. What harm was there in a mechanical device? Couldn't he play along with her on this? It went against his grain, but if it kept her happy and on an even keel, it was probably a small price to pay.

With great trepidation he Velcroed on the battery-powered contraption she proffered. It had straps and wrapped around the base of his limp penis.

"Turn it on, turn it on," urged Doris.

Saying a little prayer, he switched on the starter button. He didn't realize there were three speeds. Inadvertently, he'd hit "high." The jiggling was quick and strong and frightening. His poor penis felt as if it were being mauled. He shut it off.

"Doris, that was not enjoyable. I tried it. You saw me. Now, put it away. Get it out of my sight." He ripped it off.

Doris laughed. She'd been watching intently.

"Wait, you hit the wrong speed, that's all. Press 'Low,' then move it up a notch when you're ready. Trust me, it feels wonderful. Do it," she commanded.

Unwilling to start the day with a major disagreement, Jake gritted his teeth and fiddled with the straps of the vibrator again. When it was in place, he pressed "Low."

A slow, steady pulsing enveloped his member. It was not

unpleasant. In spite of himself, he lay back and let the motion have its way. He closed his eyes. She was right. It felt good. His harnessed shaft swelled and swayed. It grew hard and firm. He pushed the button up a level. The vibration increased accordingly. Doris put a Kleenex in his hand. He was going, going, gone! He spurted into the tissue. Ah so!

And so, to his surprise, Jake was initiated into the world of mechanical devices. In the years that ensued, the vibrators got bigger and bumpier. They bought and watched porno films together. The films got raunchier and raunchier. For his birthday one year, Doris presented him with a penis enhancer. Jake had a few problems with that to start, but after a while he got the hang of it and enjoyed brandishing his new equipment. He didn't mean to, but sometimes he frightened his wife. That only seemed to heighten the excitement. By and large, their sex life was quite satisfactory. They were bonded to the max. It was their little secret. Besides, who would have believed it?

◆ ◆ ◆

This particular Thursday morn, Doris woke Jake up with a little kiss on the cheek and a decidedly vicious nip on the ear. With a yelp, he opened his eyes to see Doris already out of bed and rummaging through her toy drawer. As she pulled out her newest plaything, he sat upright and announced firmly, "Not now, I told you Mike Hannagan was due at ten. We have to get dressed. Behave yourself."

"Why is he coming here? We have things to do. He's getting to be a real pest, always hanging around, annoying the help," sulked Doris.

"You know damn well what he's doing. I don't understand your attitude. This isn't a game we're playing. You know the score. The sooner he nails the crooks, the better off we'll be. Let's not antagonize him. He's on our side. Business isn't so wonderful lately, or haven't you noticed?"

Jake got out of bed and headed for the bathroom. Doris

made a face at his retreating back, folded up a peculiar harness, and put it back in the drawer.

They were at the kitchen table, finishing their coffee when Hannagan rang the doorbell promptly at ten o'clock. Jake greeted him and ushered him into a small, walnut-paneled study. Tawny leather armchairs and a small matching sofa blended into the background. On the floor, an unusual muted cinnamon, cream, and brick red Oriental claimed Mike's attention. He asked Jake about the carpet.

"It's a Turkish Melas," he replied, "a prayer rug. You have a good eye." Jake had noticed and was amused by Mike's aptitude for rugs. He called Doris to join them.

Doris and Jake settled themselves on the pliant leather sofa. Mike sat across from them. He began carefully.

"First of all, I want to thank you. I've never been around or known anything about Oriental rugs. It's a great learning experience and I'm getting a hoot out of it. I think I can understand how a person would feel if a rug he or she loved suddenly disappeared. I'd be bullshit. Excuse me, ma'am."

Doris studied Mike as he spoke. His words seemed sincere. Could it be this policeman or detective or whoever he was really liked rugs? That would be something! She interrupted him.

"Would you like to see our rugs? Come on, I'll give you the tour. We have some beauties, very rare. I've been collecting for years."

To Jake's astonishment, Mike and Doris got up and wandered off, leaving Jake to read the newspaper. From time to time and from a distance, he caught snatches of the lecture Doris was delivering. Half an hour passed. Jake went looking for them.

He found them in the storage room in the basement. Doris had unfolded two or three of her treasures, all Kazaks, and was lovingly describing their origin and history to Mike, who appeared to be enthralled. Jake was getting aggravated. He was thinking: Some detective, he's never going to crack this case. He's wasting time—mine and his.

But Mike Hannagan was working hard. He needed Doris as an ally, and he was trying to make it happen. He was interested in her rugs, all right, but he was more interested in gaining her confidence. She had to trust him. She had a fondness for every piece in her collection. They were all very dear to her. When she told him that the remainder of her hoard was stockpiled in a warehouse in Somerville, he asked if she'd show them to him. Doris was pleased. She said that Jake took care of the warehouse. She'd never stepped foot in the place, but she was sure it wasn't a problem. She'd get the keys. They were trying to fix a date when Jake broke into their discussion.

"Listen you two, forget Somerville. We've got problems and they're not in Somerville. How about some action in Boston? Is that too much to ask?"

Now Hannagan was annoyed. This was the first he'd heard of a warehouse. He didn't like surprises. Another piece of the puzzle? He asked Jake if the warehouse was just for personal storage, Doris's rugs. Jake admitted he also kept some overstock from the store there.

"How do you know which is which?" asked Mike.

"Don't worry, I know the difference," grumbled Jake.

At this moment, Mike caught Doris eyeing her husband. If looks could kill, he'd be a dead man. What was that about? Mike wondered.

"God help you if you ever touch one of my rugs," said Doris grimly.

To break the tension, Hannagan took out his small notebook and suggested they go back to the library. He wanted to go over each of the robberies with them again. He needed to fill in some background stuff.

Another hour went by. Doris had a story for every stolen carpet on the list: the Potters' Tabriz; the Hutchins's Bakhtiari; the Seders' Sarouk . . . Mike learned that the Seagulls had a semi-social relationship with many of their customers stemming from the unique service they offered. They made professional visits to advise on the selection and placement of rugs from CD. That was service, thought Mike. As it happened, in the last twelve months, they had been entertained in the homes of all eight of the victims. Did that mean anything?

Doris asked Mike if he'd like some coffee. He never refused. She left the room.

Jake took the opportunity to advise Hannagan about his wife's nervous condition, how he tried to downplay stressful situations. He warned the detective not to expect too much from Doris. In other words, hands off.

Now more than ever, Mike was convinced that Doris was the key. But the key to what? She knew more than she was saying.

Doris arrived with the coffee. They chatted for a few more minutes. Mike thanked them for their time, excused himself, and left, telling Doris he was looking forward to seeing the rest of her collection soon.

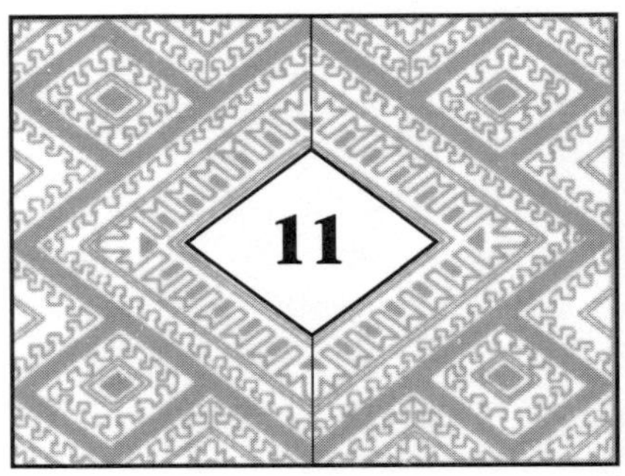

Today Sarah was not working. She was at the sink in her sunny blue and white kitchen rinsing the breakfast dishes. The daily hubbub of the morning rush was over. Martin was at work; the children were on their way to school. She was thinking about her husband's unexpected invitation to join him on a trip to Santa Fe. It was business for him. He was scheduled to speak at a lawyers' conference there. For her it would be a vacation. She'd always wanted to see New Mexico. So what if his colleagues were stuffy and dull. She didn't have to stay with the group. She would have to call Classic Design to make arrangements. The Seagulls probably wouldn't mind. It had been very slow at the store lately. Martin said his mother would be happy to stay with the children. He had it all figured out.

Why now?

For years he'd been attending the annual meetings of the Defense Investigative Foundation (D.I.F.) by himself. She'd wanted to go, but he'd always had one excuse or another to deal her out. Now that she'd lost interest in his trips, he was inviting her. Such was life, she sighed.

Two weeks later, Sarah and Martin were checking into the

Eldorado Hotel in downtown Santa Fe. Sarah was dismayed by the luxuriously bland atmosphere. The deluxe contemporary southwestern inn was not what she expected. A concierge desk yet! They could be anywhere. So much for picturesque old New Mexico!

Preparations hadn't gone well. Martin wasn't much fun. Instead of drawing them closer, the trip seemed to have widened the gap. For no good reason.

Sarah had taken out two or three library books on Santa Fe. Research was her favorite pastime. She was going to love the place, she knew already. She tried to share her enthusiasm with Martin.

"We should drive up to Abaquiu to Georgia O'Keeffe territory and see the Pedernal, her special mountain that looms large in so many of her paintings. I'm crazy about her work. I wonder if her house is open to the public? How about Taos? I'd love to see Mabel Dodge Luhan's place. She was a character."

"The planning committee has made all the arrangements, Sarah. Just leave it at that. There won't be time for your esoteric pilgrimages. You might consider me and try a little diplomatic socializing for once. It wouldn't hurt. Why do you always go off on tangents?"

Because that's who I am, thought Sarah. You don't have a clue.

They'd even had words about the clothes she was taking. According to the travel guides, Santa Fe was blue-jeans casual. She was assembling her denims and T-shirts when Martin intercepted.

"Be sure you take some fancy outfits. There's a formal dinner dance Saturday night and a kick-off cocktail party Wednesday evening. I'm taking my tux. Your black lace dress would be fine."

"Are you serious? You said this was going to be fun and relaxing. I don't want to drag that stuff. I'll take a skirt and a couple of nice blouses. That should do."

"Sarah, the women dress up at these affairs. Nobody wears

blue jeans, not even during the day. Do me a favor, take a couple of your pretty evening outfits. Why are you so perverse?"

Martin had finally noticed his wife's disaffection. He couldn't understand it. What did she have to be unhappy about? Women! The more they had, the more they wanted. The trip was a goodwill gesture on his part, a gesture that was already fizzling. What was the matter with her? She was going to spoil everything.

In their tastefully appointed hotel room, they unpacked, freshened up, and headed out the door, he to check the program schedule downstairs, she to the Plaza and the Governor's Palace and La Fonda for starters. They'd agreed to meet back in the hotel lobby in two hours.

Sarah hurried up the main street to the parklike plaza that was the heart of the city. The sun was shining brightly, the day was dry and clear. The Sangre de Cristo Mountains stood guard to the east. And there it was!

Against the front of the adobe Governor's Palace, a long line of blankets stretched out on the sidewalk, each one attended by a Native American sitting with his or her display of handcrafted silver and turquoise jewelry. Just like the pictures in the books. According to the captions, they were from the Santa Domingo Pueblo south of the city. What a photo opportunity! In her haste, Sarah had forgotten her camera. Rats! But she'd be back.

Strolling quickly past the tempting array of native American jewelry, she resolved to do her shopping early the next morning. Then she cut diagonally across the plaza to the legendary La Fonda.

She knew there were newer and nicer hotels in the area, but for sheer color and ambiance, the inn at the end of the Santa Fe Trail did it for Sarah. It was love at first sight: the pueblolike structure, the lobby right out of the old West, the tacky little shops. She stopped at one, Señor Murphy's, for a bag of pine nuts to nibble. The preponderance of art galleries around the plaza astounded her. Look at all the people!

A walking tour was what she needed to get her bearings. She remembered reading about one that originated at La Fonda. Perfect. She found the tour desk and signed up for the 10:00 A.M. tour the next day. A glance at her watch told her she was running late. Martin would be furious.

When she returned to the Eldorado, she found Martin sitting in the lobby with two lawyer friends. (There was no mistaking them.)

"Here she is, my long-lost wife. Sarah, I'd like you to meet Steve Petersen and Mel Winn. Would you like a cold drink or would you rather go up and rest? Their wives have gone up to change for the cocktail party. You must be tired; we've been up since dawn."

"I'd love a tall glass of iced tea. I'm really thirsty. Must be the altitude. I'm happy to meet you, gentlemen. No, I'm not the least bit tired, just excited about being in Santa Fe. Have you been here before?" she asked the men.

Martin's companions admitted that although they'd attended three or four conferences in New Mexico, they hadn't seen or done much. They were always too busy, too programmed. Besides, sightseeing was woman's work.

Okay, thought Sarah, I'm on my own. I'm going to see and do as much as I can cram into these few days. Martin will have to make excuses for me. Good thing he's so preoccupied, but that's his normal state.

First thing the next morning, Sarah trotted over to the Governor's Palace to peruse the sidewalk jewelry display. She bought silver bracelets for her two little daughters and a silver belt buckle for her son. For herself, she chose long, dangling liquid silver earrings and a handsome, chunky turquoise and silver necklace. After the walking tour, which was interesting and fun, Sarah felt comfortable roaming about on her own. It was an easy city.

She knew there'd be no time for Abaquiu, but the Museum of Fine Arts had a decent collection of O'Keeffes, which she enjoyed thoroughly. The history and artifacts as presented inside the Governor's Palace made her long for her son, who was a nut about the old West. She bought him two large books at the sales desk. On the way back to the hotel to drop off the heavy books, she happened into the posh Elaine Horwitch Gallery. It was a sleek and dazzling space filled with paintings and sculpture and jewelry and amusing objets d'art. Impressive but not her style, decided Sarah.

That same afternoon Sarah discovered the gallery that did please her. Everything about the Fenn Galleries appealed to her: the rambling, old adobe building, the cool, dark interior, the old paintings hung alongside the new paintings, the amazing ethnic jewelry. She almost missed the best part of all, the garden with its exotic fish pond and life-sized sculptures. Luckily a salesperson suggested she visit the grounds. Sarah stepped outside and into another world. It was peaceful and perfect, this al fresco exhibit. She sat down on a stone bench to ponder the wonders of nature and man. She was mesmerized. Time passed.

With a start, she was roused by the chatter of some people entering her sanctuary. She got up and did a quick tour of the garden, stopping briefly to admire each sculpture. *The Puddle Jumpers* by Glenna Goodacre, a study in bronze of a group of children caught in mid-air, made her laugh. An elderly couple sitting quietly on a bench, lifelike in every detail down to the Ferragamo pumps on the woman's feet, made her smile. She touched the woman's shoulder just to make sure she wasn't real. Martin had to see this! Actually, she wished Jon were here. He would appreciate it.

She was late getting back to the hotel, and Martin, as usual, was annoyed.

"Where have you been all day?"

She ignored his question and countered with, "How did your speech go?"

It took him fifteen minutes to describe the enthusiastic reception his talk had received and all the questions he'd fielded and how favorable the comments had been. He was well pleased but not with her.

"Martin, since tonight is a free night, I was hoping we might drive up to Rancho de Chimayo for dinner, the two of us. It's not far, and I've heard it's very romantic. I have the directions. Please?"

"Sarah, this is business. I've already made reservations at the Bull Ring. We're eating with the Petersens and the Winns. They're important to me. You could help by chatting with the women and letting the men talk shop. Is that too much to ask?"

"Yes, if you want to know. What am I doing here? You invited me. Obviously you'd be much happier by yourself. Admit it."

"Okay. I thought you'd enjoy seeing how I operate. I was wrong. I won't ask you again, believe me."

Both of them were angry. The gulf between them seemed unbreachable. Sarah thought she'd had enough. Martin thought, Who needed this aggravation? What happened to my docile, sweet wife? The silence in the room was ominous.

Sarah was nearing her breaking point. Two nights in a row, Martin had rebuffed her sexual advances. Feeling more confident in that department, thanks to her playtime with Jon, she had bathed, perfumed, donned her sexiest nightgown, and vamped her husband. Little good it did. When she'd climbed into his queen-sized bed (there were two to a room) to kiss and nuzzle him goodnight, he hadn't responded. When she'd reached playfully for his precious male organ, he'd slapped her hand away.

Now she was weighing the pros and cons of life without Martin. The children? No, he wouldn't claim the children. That was woman's work, and he was a very busy man. The children would be lucky to see him now and then. They'd be upset. That was a given. Could she work full time? Probably. The house? He wouldn't want the kids uprooted. Could she handle everything herself? Not likely. Sarah began to tremble.

"Martin, you'll have to make excuses for me. I'm not feeling well. Say it's the altitude or whatever you want to say. I'll order up a sandwich from room service."

With that Sarah rushed into the bathroom, slammed the

door, sank down on the travertine marble floor, her back against the tub, and wept into a thick terry bath towel that she hoped would muffle the sound.

Martin stared after her. Now what? She was really annoying him. He wished she hadn't come, that he hadn't invited her. She was a big nuisance. How long was she planning to stay in the bathroom? He had to shower and change. He started to pace. Ten minutes went by. He rapped on the bathroom door.

"Sarah, are you all right? I've got to shower. Could you come out of there? We—I'm due at the Bull Ring at seven thirty."

When Sarah realized that Martin wasn't the least bit interested or concerned about her feelings, she threw in the towel. She splashed cold water on her face, brushed back her frizzy mane, took a deep breath, and opened the door.

Martin, looking agitated, was standing in the middle of the room. His change of clothes was laid out neatly on the bed. "You know I'm in a hurry. You have no consideration. What can you be thinking?" It was his turn to slam the door as he entered the bathroom.

Sarah picked up the phone and asked for the concierge. She inquired about the next available flight to Boston and about transportation to the Albuquerque airport, jotting down the information on the little pad of paper at bedside. She was going home. She got her suitcase out of the closet, opened it on her bed, and started throwing her things into it. By the time Martin came out of the bathroom, she was almost packed.

Startled by the suitcase and the look on his wife's face, he stopped in his tracks. She brushed past him to collect her toiletries from the bathroom. As she stuffed her cosmetics and odds and ends into her case, he came to his senses.

"Where do you think you're going?" he demanded.

"Home, where I won't be in your way. Martin, we have to talk but not here. You finish your meetings and come home. I have something important to say to you."

He didn't like the firm, determined tone of her voice. But

in one respect she was right. He'd be able to enjoy the rest of the conference without her. He never should have brought her. It wouldn't happen again. He'd say there was a crisis at home to explain her sudden departure. No, it wasn't a problem.

"You do as you please. Here's your ticket. You'll probably be able to exchange it for another flight. If not, use your credit card. Sarah, I'm very disappointed. You've let me down. We'll have to talk about this."

It dawned on Sarah that Martin was not angry. He was relieved to see her go. He didn't care about her anymore, she realized. She wondered if he ever had. He wanted a wife to do his bidding, and she'd outgrown that role. She hoped she knew what she was doing.

She zippered and locked her bag, then called the desk to send up a porter. Martin continued dressing. They did not speak. When there was a knock on the door, she looked at her husband sadly, then turned away.

"I'll see you Sunday," she said.

As the bus for Albuquerque headed out of Santa Fe, her immediate regrets were, oddly enough, that she hadn't been to Seret and Sons, the only indoor-outdoor rug bazaar in America. It would have been fun describing it to the gang at CD. And that she'd missed the triple crown, the three museums on the hill: the International Folk Art Museum, the Museum of Indian Arts, and the Wheelwright. She loved what little she'd seen, and she was sad about leaving. In more ways than one. She vowed to return someday. She'd had a taste of Santa Fe.

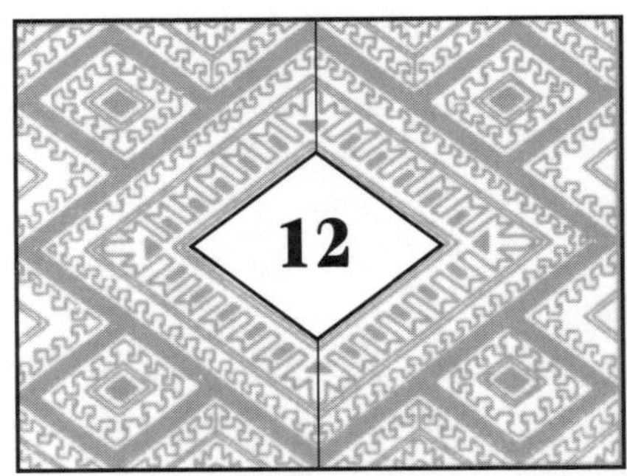


There wasn't much doing at Classic Design that week. Sarah was away, and Doris and Jake had opted for the Connecticut shore to open their summer home. That meant that Lesley, Sophie, and Jon each forfeited a day off. Once in a while it happened. Not often. The staff tried to be accommodating.

Sophie was worrying over a sheaf of papers in her hand. For want of any customers, they'd been checking inventory, a never ending chore. A small, choice Turkish Melas seemed to be missing. No one remembered its being sold. Lesley swore she saw it last week. They'd looked everywhere. Doris had in fact made off with the little rug. It was stuffed into a Lord & Taylor shopping bag on the closet shelf in her bedroom.

"Maybe Jake set it aside for someone. Let's not overreact 'til we talk to him. Rugs don't disappear," said Jon.

"Unless they're stolen," added Lesley under her breath.

Her remark made Sophie smile. There'd been no robberies at CD, thank God. Besides, given a chocolate feast, who would choose a gumdrop? If she were going to rob this store, she'd take the old Tabriz or the old Bakhtiari. Not the Melas. The rug had to be there.

"Jon, take a look downstairs in the storeroom. I can't imagine why it would be there, but maybe Jake did put it away. Do you mind?"

Jon was happy to have something to do. Without Sarah at work, the days were long and tedious. She made all the difference. He wasn't in love with her, but he did love being with her. Who wouldn't? Their fun and games had blown his mind. There was no one like Sarah.

While Jon was searching for the lost rug, Mike Hannagan walked purposefully into the store. Sophie and Lesley welcomed him warmly, but today he was all business. He had an appointment with the Seagulls at 11:30, he announced, checking his watch. He was on time. Where were they?

"They must have forgotten the date," said Sophie apologetically. "Can we help?"

Now Mike was annoyed. This was the second time they'd stood him up. Doris was anxious for him to see the rest of her collection in the warehouse. Jake was not. He made no bones about it. Why? Either he didn't want Doris—or he didn't want him to see what was there. He'd get a warrant if need be, but that was no way to handle the Seagulls. That he knew.

"How about a cup of coffee? That always helps. Where is everybody?" asked Mike.

The minute he'd walked into the place he'd missed Sarah. He was that much aware of her.

"Sarah's on vacation, and Jon is downstairs looking for a missing rug," answered Lesley. "We have a little mystery here ourselves: what happened to a Melas prayer rug?"

"Melas—that sounds familiar. Hmm. Right. I saw my first Melas at the Seagulls' a couple of weeks ago. Good looking. I wouldn't mind owning one."

"Mrs. Seagull has the best, no contest. She wanted the one we're looking for, but Jake wouldn't let her take it. They had a big fight about it," remembered Lesley.

"Maybe I won't ask Jake over the phone. I don't want to

stir up any trouble," said Sophie, thinking aloud. Damn! We spend half our time tiptoeing about. Such nonsense.

Mike made no comment. He had a theory or two about the robberies now. He wanted to be proven wrong. It was going to upset a lot of good people.

The phone rang. When Lesley picked up, she smiled and covered the mouthpiece, speaking low. Sophie, realizing what was happening, tried to distract Mike. She started quizzing him on the Orientals. It was a game he enjoyed.

"Peter, darling, we'll have to skip tomorrow. I have to work. I know. I feel the same way, but Doris and Jake are out of town, and Sarah's in Santa Fe. There's no help for it. You sound angry. Don't be. No, I can't do it. Try to understand. I'll make it up to you. Please, Peter. Yes, call me tomorrow. Goodbye."

Lesley and Peter had been meeting on a regular basis, once a week for more than a year. This would be the first break in their routine. Lesley was dismayed at Peter's angry reaction. She was not happy about skipping their rendezvous either, but what could she do? She was feeling pressured. She sighed and turned to Sophie and the rug quiz.

Mike was a quick study; it went with the job. He'd picked up much of their professional patter. He really sounded as if he knew his rugs. What was more, he was eager to learn. At the moment he was trying to describe a Sarouk but was only succeeding in making Sophie laugh.

"They're pink, and they're dyed with yogurt. I'm not sure how, but that's what Mrs. Seagull told me," said Mike.

Sophie had never heard about yogurt dyes. She'd have to check it out. It did sound funny. She never knew when Mike was kidding. Still, they got along fine.

Mike stuck around for a few more minutes. As he left, he asked Sophie to call him if the Melas turned up. He wrote down his number for her. The request puzzled Sophie, but she agreed readily. Had Mike found the connection to the thefts? Was it at CD? Sophie didn't want to know.

A few people straggled in during the afternoon. Lesley sent

out a Tibetan rug on approval. Sophie sold an odd Malayer that was very similar to a Sarouk in stock, though a tad coarser in weave and a bit more geometric in design. Jon rented out a large Persian Herez for a week, to be used in a TV movie being filmed in Boston.

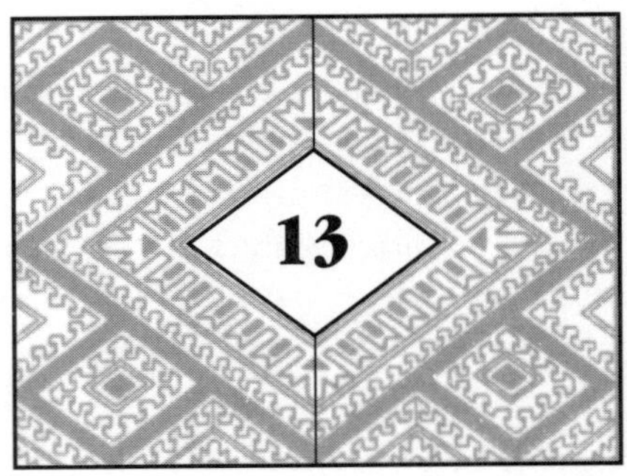


Dinnertime that evening. Jon, Nedra, and Heidi were sitting at their old pine kitchen table. It didn't happen very often. Their schedules rarely coincided. Tonight was special. They'd collaborated on a chicken cacciatore with pasta and a garden salad. Heidi had made the salad and was proud of it. For once Jon didn't have a script of a play in front of him, and Nedra was really being attentive.

"How was school today? What did you do?" asked Nedra. Heidi had been having problems at school recently, and both Nedra and Jon had met with her teacher to try to determine the reason for her poor performance in class.

"We had a history test, and I didn't know any of it. It was on the lessons we went over last night. I couldn't remember," said Heidi.

"Why not?" asked her mother. "You were right on top of it."

"I dunno," said Heidi.

Nedra and Jon looked at each other. They were unaware that Heidi and her friend Lisa, both fifth graders, were popping pills all day, pills supplied by Jimmy Ryan, the neighborhood juvenile delinquent. He was getting a kick out of seeing the little girls get high. They'd been at it for about a month. Neither one of the children dared tell her parents. For good reason. They were afraid Jimmy would get mad at them and cut off the pills, and they knew full well that their folks would punish them if they ever found out. They were feeling very grown up, and they liked the feeling.

The real trouble was school. They were either too silly or too fuzzy to concentrate. Each day went by in a blur. Tests were unthinkable. Their teachers were losing patience. It would never have occurred to any of them, knowing eleven-year-old Heidi, that pills were causing her strange behavior.

"Heidi, we'll talk about this later. You haven't even tasted the pasta. You chose the menu. What's the matter?"

"I'm not hungry. All this food is making me nauseous." Indeed, at the moment, Heidi looked pale slumped in her chair, staring at her plate. Tiny beads of sweat covered her face. "I think I'm going to throw up." Heidi ran for the bathroom.

"Jon, there's something terribly wrong with Heidi. We're taking her to the emergency room at the hospital. *Now.* Go get a blanket to wrap around her." Nedra was in a panic but was struggling to stay calm.

Jon thought his wife was overreacting, but he did what she asked. When his ashen-faced daughter finally came out of the bathroom, he hugged her, wrapped the blanket about her, picked her up, and carried her to the car. As he placed her carefully in the back seat, Heidi demanded to know where he was taking her.

"To see a doctor, honey. To make sure you're okay."

Heidi began to shriek. Nedra got in the front seat next to Jon, slammed the car door, and they were off. It was a fifteen-minute ride to the hospital, which that evening Jon made in ten. Heidi screamed the whole way.

He pulled into a parking slot in the emergency zone. He half lifted, half dragged his resistant little girl out of the car and into the hospital. By now she was hysterical and out of control. Jon was unnerved. What was wrong with his little darling? "Please God, let her be okay," he pleaded softly.

Luckily at that time, there was a lull in the emergency room traffic. A nurse directed Jon into a tiny examining room and went to fetch the intern on duty. Heidi continued to howl. Nedra stood silently, watching her daughter. Jon tried to comfort the child.

When the intern arrived, he motioned the parents out of the cubicle and drew the partitioning curtain.

Jon and Nedra went to the waiting room and sat down. Heidi's outburst had been so unexpected that both of them were stunned. Two people totally immersed in themselves, in their own search for identity and recognition, were being jolted back to reality. Something was the matter with their adorable child. What could it be? They were at a loss.

The minutes dragged by. An hour passed. Finally the young intern appeared. He assured them that Heidi would be all right. They'd pumped out her stomach and done a toxicology blood screen. They could take her home soon.

"But what's wrong, what happened?" asked Nedra tearfully.

"She's been taking pills, all kinds of garbage—Dexedrine, Xanax, and Librium for starters. It's a wonder she isn't sicker. She said her friend Lisa is doing it too. Eleven years old! It's criminal. I have the name of the little creep who's been giving them the stuff. Jimmy Ryan. Don't you ever look at her? The eyes—look at her eyes. I hate to see children getting hooked. It turns my stomach."

Fairly or unfairly, the intern laid the blame squarely on the parents. He admonished them for several more minutes, then walked out abruptly.

Nedra was crying; Jon was grim-faced. "I'll kill the bastard," he threatened.

"He's right," said Nedra. "We're both so busy that we hardly notice what she's doing just as long as she doesn't make waves. We give her everything except our time and undivided attention. Jon, it's a warning! We've got to change." Nedra blew her nose and wiped her eyes.

Jon nodded in agreement. He thought of all the time he'd wasted putting together his wardrobe and fooling around in the theater. Like a kid who loved to dress up and be on stage. Was the rush he got from applause like the rush from drugs? But Heidi was a baby! She was *his* baby. Jon was distraught.

They sat quietly, each agonizing over his or her shortcomings and vowing to make it up to Heidi. More time passed. At last a nurse came in to tell them Heidi was ready to go home.

It was a very quiet, subdued family that returned home. Heidi was still nauseous from the hospital procedure. Nedra told her she could skip school the next day and stay in bed. She gave her a Popsicle to suck and sent her to wash up and put on her pajamas. Jon was champing at the bit, anxious to confront the Ryans. Nedra cautioned him to wait awhile. She picked up the phone and called the Parkers, Lisa's folks. As calmly and succinctly as she could, she described the situation to them, explaining what the doctor had said. When she hung up, she told Jon that the two families would confront the Ryans together.

◆ ◆ ◆

The encounter with the Ryans was anything but pleasant. The father, a belligerent, red-faced owner of a local barroom, was indignant and angry. The mother seemed fearful. When they called in their son, he denied everything at first. But then his father pinned him against the wall, twisting his arm. He screamed out in pain. Yes, he'd been giving pills to the little girls. For fun. No hard stuff. What was the harm? His father told him loud and clear.

Mr. Ryan took off his belt, and holding his son with one arm, began to whip him slowly and methodically. The Parkers and the Hedstroms exited hurriedly, Jimmy's wails ringing in their ears.

For Jon nothing would ever be the same. His Heidi. He had to be there for her. She needed a mother and a father. The fun and games were over. All the extracurricular activities. His sexual fantasies were fading fast too. Sarah would understand; they were really good buddies. The heat had been turned down. Life happened.

Nedra had few illusions. Her dream of becoming a full professor was simply a dream. Not enough time, not enough energy. Heidi was her number-one priority now. Whatever it took, she and Jon would work it out. They had to.

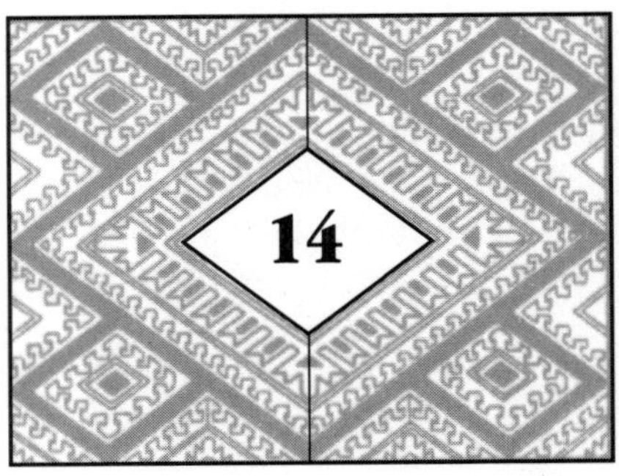


On the way home from work, Lesley stopped at the Legal Seafood Market in Chestnut Hill to pick up some fresh fish for dinner. The salmon looked particularly good. She decided quickly on a meal of poached salmon, boiled new red potatoes, and sauteed sugarsnap peas with a green salad. Because Ken loved their salt breadsticks, she added half a dozen to her order as a special treat. She picked up a ripe honeydew melon and a pint of lime sorbet to top it off. That settled, she gathered her food together, checked it out, and lugged the heavy grocery bag to her car.

From there it was a short drive to her home in Wellesley. Although she'd worked the whole day, Lesley felt pleasantly relaxed and was looking forward to a quiet evening with Ken. Usually she shifted into high gear as she approached her house. For the last few months she'd been a virtual whirling dervish, preparing dinner, straightening up the kitchen, setting a pretty table. By the time Ken got home, having changed and freshened her makeup, she was the very model of the perfect housewife. At a price.

She hauled her groceries into the kitchen and looked around in dismay. The remains of breakfast were still in the sink; the kitchen needed attention. As she stowed the salmon in the refrigerator and put the sorbet in the freezer, an open bottle of white table wine caught her eye. She took a wineglass from the cupboard and poured herself a hefty drink. Then she tackled the dirty dishes and the kitchen cleanup, pausing every now and then for a sip of wine.

Humming her favorite Strauss waltz and sipping from her second glass of wine, she was preparing the sugarsnaps when Ken walked in. She was startled when he grabbed her about the waist and waltzed her around the kitchen, all the while whistling the same lilting tune. Too soon the music stopped because they were both laughing and out of breath. They hadn't shared such a spontaneous moment in a long, long time. They eyed each other thoughtfully.

"That was quite an entrance. Supper's not ready yet. I seem to be working in slow motion. Must be the wine. Have some, it's not bad," offered Lesley, filling another glass for her husband.

"Don't hurry, Lesley. It's good to see you relaxed. You've been so compulsive and jittery lately. I worry about you."

"Do you?" said Lesley. "Sometimes I think you forget I live here. What I mean is that you seem to be living in another world. By yourself."

"Lesley, we've gone the distance. Good times, bad times. We've managed to survive. I do take you for granted. You're the ballast in my life. When I had to close the plant last year and take a job as a sales rep, I was on shaky ground. I didn't know what the future would hold, or if I even had a future. I've been totally self-absorbed. How do you put up with me? It's not fair, I give you, but that's how it is."

Right after his college graduation, Ken had gone to work in his family's shoe business, which manufactured inexpensive work shoes for men and women. His father had opened the factory in the thirties. It was a great American success story for many years. But things changed, and the shoe industry fell upon hard times. It was left to Ken to suffer the losses and finally to call a halt. He was grateful that his father did not live long enough to see the demise of his dream. He was also grateful that his children were educated and that the mortgage on his house was paid. He still had terrible guilt about his long-term employees, now unemployed, and his father's name, which was no longer golden. The last few years had been difficult.

"What you and I need, Lesley, is a vacation. Things are going well. Who knew I'd turn out to be a salesman? Let's plan a trip."

Lesley was momentarily overcome. She took another sip of wine. Ken's forthright admission had taken her by surprise. So typical of Ken. Unable to communicate, trying to spare her his pain, shutting himself off until he'd licked his wounds, leaving her in the dark. Damn it! Look at the damage that had been done. And there was Peter. She really cared about him. She was not a frivolous woman, but she did seem to have the equivalent of two husbands to worry about. Good Lord!

"Ken, supper's almost ready. Go wash up. We'll talk."

And talk they did. They talked through dinner and dessert. The food was perfect. They talked until the tall, flickering candles had burned down to short stumps. They were still talking when Lesley glanced at her watch.

"Ken, it's eleven o'clock! Tomorrow is a work day. What happened? Where did the time go?"

"Lesley, I have a few more things to say to you. Come on, we'll do the dishes together. Then we'll adjourn to the bedroom."

They were like young lovers that night. He was strong and sure and very tender with her. She was more responsive than she had ever been, loving him with her mouth, her tongue, her whole being. She was on top of him, at his side, under him. Her sex was wet. He dipped his fingers into it, rubbing her clitoris. They knew how to push each other's buttons. Taking their own sweet time, they played together, some old tricks and some new, until the ride was uncontrollable. Afterwards they lay panting, satisfied and well pleased with themselves, so unlike their recent sporadic and unrewarding lovemaking.

"Sweetheart, if I were a younger man or in better shape," laughed Ken, "but I'm not and that's it. I've shot my load. Not too shabby, was I? Lesley, have I told you how much I love you? After all these years, I feel the same way. How do you put up with me? I'm moody, difficult, and uncommunicative."

Lesley, cuddling at his side, thought, And I'm unfaithful. What a combo! She had hardly suffered a pang of guilt over her relationship with Peter. She'd wondered about that. Obviously she'd been justifying Ken's total withdrawal from her by acting out her own agenda. She'd fallen for Peter. And she loved Ken. I'm really screwed up, she decided, trying not to panic. She needed help.

"Shush, Ken, you were magnificent tonight. But why you insist upon putting yourself through such torture in what amounts to solitary confinement is beyond me. I felt as if you had left me, that you didn't care. How was I to know what you were going through? Ken, I love you, but you're also impossible."

Now what? Could she handle all this? She could try. Face it, she had no intention of giving Peter up. He made her feel young. Of course, the mechanics of the affair were time-consuming and near-comical, especially at her age. It was the maintenance. She was spending more time shaving her legs and bleaching her upper lip than she had ever thought possible. Her hairdresser had become her best friend. Lunch hours were spent racing about doing errands so that her day off would be free to dally with Peter. She'd had to skip a day off this week because the Seagulls and Sarah were away. No Peter this week. He wasn't happy, but she had a chance to catch her breath. She needed to *think*.

Ken had fallen asleep at her side. Lesley tossed and turned all night. No solution.

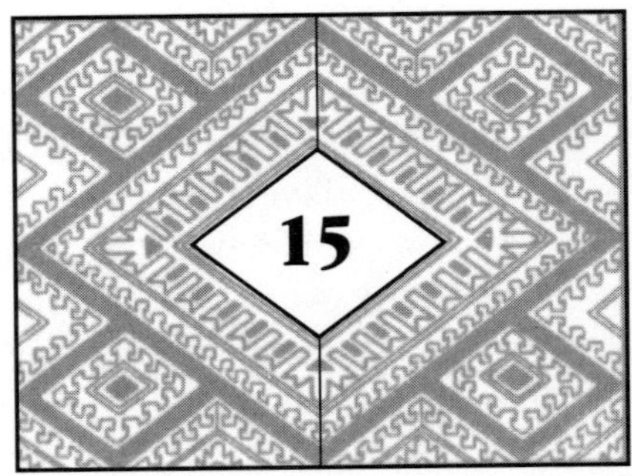

On Wednesday, the week after the debacle in Santa Fe, Sarah was at the coffee place two blocks from CD. Seated at a small, round marble table, staring into an empty cup, she was lost in thought. The sad, perplexed expression on her face discouraged any friendly intrusion. She was contemplating life as a single parent, and the prospects were depressing. The trip had convinced her that change was inevitable. She and Martin didn't work together. The children! She had to think of the children. She was frightened. A big sigh escaped her.

She was so concentrated on her problem that she didn't notice Mike Hannagan at the counter, ordering coffee. He saw her and was about to call out a greeting, but her bleak face stopped him short. *That* was misery. From his vantage point, he watched Sarah. She was going through some kind of hell, that much he could see. If he offered to help, he'd be buying the problem. His better judgment said Walk away! Mind your own business. But his feeling for Sarah got the better of him. Maybe he could help. He walked over to her table and scrunched down into the narrow chair opposite her.

"Hi! You look like you could use a friend. Try me. I've heard every story in the book. Nothing fazes me."

Mike's sudden appearance at such close range gave Sarah a start. As she brought him into focus, she realized she was relieved, even happy to see him. He looked so solid.

"Hi yourself! It's not my best day. I'm mulling over some bad stuff." Tears welled up. She swallowed hard. She would not go to pieces. She would *not.* She dabbed at her eyes with the paper napkin.

"What you need is an objective ear, which happens to be my best feature. Come on, let's take a walk." He pulled Sarah to her feet and led her out of the store.

Mike steered her firmly by the elbow toward the Public Gardens, the oasis in the middle of the city where the famous old swan boats plied their way back and forth across the picturesque pond. The flowers and trees were lush and fragrant. They walked the paths in silence at first. Eventually, Sarah took note of her companion and her surroundings. She was not even sure how she had gotten there.

"I thought the fresh air would do you good. You looked a little peaked. You were sitting at Starbuck's. Remember?"

She did. Her all-consuming dilemma again. She didn't want to burden anyone with her problem. On the other hand, she could use the feedback from an impartial third person. So be it—Mike Hannagan it was.

"Everything I say is confidential. Okay?" Mike nodded.

Sarah started hesitantly. She told him about her early years: her Catholic education, her coming to Boston, her meeting Martin the first year of college. She described their marriage: the beginning, the babies, the growing disenchantment. She tried to explain how and why she felt like an accessory instead of a full-fledged partner in their relationship. As she heard herself speak, her heart sank. She wondered if anyone would understand her. Did she sound like a whiner? Mike's face was inscrutable.

She went on. She talked about her inability to interest her husband in the pleasures of sex and her subsequent education in same. (She did not name her obliging partner. For a moment it occurred to Sarah that Mike might know about her liaison with Jon. A definite possibility. If so, it couldn't be helped.) Finally, she got to the disastrous Santa Fe trip and the exhausting, ongoing aftermath. The terrible confrontations. She didn't know if she had the strength to make a move. What did Mike think?

Mike was hardly an indifferent bystander. Having previously checked out her background for his investigation, he knew that she was on the level. One hundred percent. He struggled for a response. He was not much attuned to independent women. What did she want? Sarah was obviously suffering, but from what? It was not within Hannagan's ken to sympathize with this problem. With *Sarah,* yes. But with her need for self-fulfillment, no. He tightened his grip on her arm as if to reassure her.

"I think that life is too short to waste it being unhappy. If two people can't get along, maybe it's time to cut loose. But . . . there are children here. That's another story. You owe them. You have to explore every means of keeping their home together. What about a marriage counselor? Is that acceptable? Sarah, do you understand what you would be giving up? Do you?"

He underestimated that Sarah was suffering over *every* conceivable possibility. The end result was always the same. Social status, material things, the fine trimmings—they weren't worth the daily humiliations. Martin just didn't get it. He'd probably resist counseling, but who knew? The children would be okay, she'd see to that. If only she could find the courage to get out.

What she said was, "It's a trade-off, Mike. You lose some things, you gain others. The kids will be better off in the long run. They won't have to watch their parents whittle away at each other. They won't have to take sides or referee or tiptoe around. It's for the best."

She tried to sound confident. She looked anything but. Mike felt like putting his arms around her to comfort her. He resisted his gut reaction. He knew that was the last thing she wanted. She had to stand on her own two feet. Who was he to say no? It was a different world.

"How about a ride on a swan boat?" Mike asked, changing the subject. "I've always wanted to do that. Looks like fun."

"It does, doesn't it? I'll have to take a rain check. Believe it or not, I'm supposed to be working today. I was so blue that Sophie sent me out for a walk. Mike, you're a sweet man. It helps to talk. A lot."

She looked at him gratefully. His stern facade would never again intimidate her. What a *nice* man.

"I'll walk you back to the store. There's always the chance I'll catch the Seagulls. They've been avoiding me lately," said Mike.

"They're still in Connecticut. Today's not your day."

Mike disagreed. Walking with Sarah to CD, Mike sensed that she was feeling less troubled. Their time together had helped. At least she trusted him. It was a start.

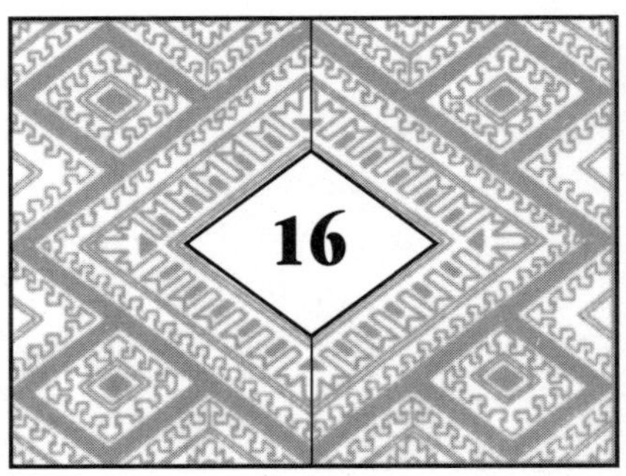


No one at CD was surprised to see Mike trailing Sarah as she walked through the door. Big hellos from the crew.

"Mike, come see this new Turkish folk art rug. It's wild," called Sophie from the back of the store.

"Any news?" This from Lesley.

"Pretty soon now," Mike assured her as he headed toward Sophie.

"Sarah, where've you been? I was beginning to worry. Are you all right?" asked Jon.

"Sorry, I shouldn't have stayed out so long. I'm not dealing with a full deck these days," apologized Sarah.

Jon nodded. He understood too well. Since the episode with Heidi, he'd been struggling over what to do and how to do it. So far, no easy answers.

The two friends somehow sensed each other's predicament. They were at a crossroads. One wrong move, and . . . they weren't sure what. The intimate games they'd played were over. They were looking at real life. They sat together, companionably close and mutually miserable.

Mike, standing next to Sophie, was scratching his head as he gazed down at the unusual rug spread out on the floor.

"What is it? Look at the giraffe and the children and the duck pond. Do I see a seesaw? Don't tell me this is an Oriental."

Sophie laughed. The brightly colored, whimsical rug amused her. She liked it. It was too much money, but she knew it would sell.

"It's a folk rug, Mike. From Turkey. Primitive but sturdy. Perfect for a ski house or a winter hideaway. Don't be stuffy."

Mike was disapproving. He had a new regard for fine rugs. As yet, he could brook no aberrations. A true convert.

"Lighten up, Mike. It's fun, playful. By the way, Jake called. If tomorrow at eleven a.m. is okay with you, they'll meet you here and take you to the warehouse. He doesn't sound too anxious," she added. "My guess is that Doris is driving him batty."

◆ ◆ ◆

*Batty* was putting it mildly. Doris had been raising hell! Jake had borne the brunt of it. He'd tried every delaying tactic he could muster.

In the two weeks since Doris had mentioned the warehouse to Mike, Jake had made three furtive trips there with Rahshi, trying to reorganize the contents of the storeroom. For years he'd been dipping into her hoard unabashedly, selling off a minor treasure or two every now and then. He watched the numbers carefully at CD. If business were off, he'd choose judiciously from the warehouse treasury, then sell a handpicked rug for big bucks. His system was infallible, he thought. Classic Design had an enviable track record. But he'd made serious inroads in her collection. After some tedious juggling he'd nervously agreed to a visit. Would she notice what was missing? With her eagle eye? Of course she would. He was not a happy host.

◆ ◆ ◆

The next day they met at the store at eleven. Mike opted to follow them to Somerville in his own beat-up Chevy. Fifteen minutes later Jake was unpadlocking his storage unit in the converted old red brick mill building. He reached in and switched on the single naked light bulb dangling from the ceiling. Doris and Mike followed him into the small, square space.

Doris gasped. There were rugs thrown about everywhere in no semblance of order.

"Jake, what a *mess*! How can I show Mike anything? You've gotten the store rugs mixed up with my collection. I've warned you about that. You never listen to me. Where is my old Tabriz? Damn you, I'm furious! You're lucky Mike is here as a buffer."

On the other hand, Jake observed morosely, you wouldn't be here if Hannagan hadn't insisted.

"Cool down, Doris. Your rugs are here. You just have to look for them. Here's the antique Tabriz and the Bidjar. There's the Shirvan. Don't stand around, come on, show Mike."

Then to Jake's everlasting surprise, his wife motioned Mike to a perch on top of some rugs. She dug into the nearest stack, turning up corners, describing the rugs and their history. With a good deal of help from Jake, she was able to move her own rugs front and center. She never said a word about the missing pieces. She carried on as if nothing were wrong. She even seemed cheerful.

Jake knew intuitively that Doris knew. She'd always been miserly about her precious Orientals. So faced with his obvious double-dealing, why was she calm? Something was brewing.

He'd dreaded this day. Maybe she was holding back because of Mike. No, that wasn't her style. She didn't care who witnessed her outbursts. He caught her watching him out of the corner of her eye. Cat-who-swallowed-the-canary look.

She was not an easy read today. Jake prided himself in

anticipating her every mood. That was what had attracted Doris in the first place: his clear, unequivocal devotion to her. Other young men had sought her favors, but they were aggressive and demanding. No, Jake suited her fine. For thirty-five years he'd watched over her carefully, if surreptitiously. Since that day long ago when he'd promised her father, the formidable Meyer O. Mintz, that he would take care of his beloved daughter, he'd kept his word. (In Jake's book, selling off her rugs didn't count.) He knew from the start that his father-in-law didn't like him. Jake didn't have much to offer Doris: no money, no social standing. Still, he was well educated (Boston University, full scholarship) and pleasant to look at, if a trifle pudgy. He had a future. Strange man, that Meyer. His reputation was horrendous. Jake didn't believe most of it. Why should he? The man was soft-spoken and polite with him. (Jake's own hardworking father, the owner and mainstay of a small grocery store, had warned him about Meyer O. Mintz. Mintz was bad news. Stay clear!)

But Jake had fallen for Doris. She was good-looking, smart, and sure of herself. He found her self-confidence very appealing. That was not his long suit. She bolstered his morale. He could hardly believe his good fortune when she agreed to marry him. The fact that she came with her own income (funds set up by her doting dad) was an unexpected boon, or so he thought. He learned quickly that Doris didn't share. (The only child syndrome?) Jake had to buckle down and earn a living. Still Doris was an enthusiastic working partner in Classic Design. She put some money into it at the start and realized a handsome profit. For years the store had provided them a good living, one way or another. Doris did what she pleased with her own money. She was worth a bundle now, Jake knew that. In his way, Jake adored the woman and considered himself a lucky devil to be her mate. And life was *never* dull with Doris.

Jake listened to his wife's commentary on an unusual kilim. He marveled at her knowledge.

Mike was trying to concentrate on the lecture. The slipshod

condition of the storage unit bothered him. So unlike the perfect order of the store. Rahshi told him last week that he had been helping Jake in Somerville. The clutter had to be deliberate! Mike didn't know enough about Orientals to tell which rugs were which. The elaborate subterfuge was for Doris's benefit. She was on to Jake. Doris knew what was going on. She had the answers.

Mike interrupted Doris with a question about a rug.

Doris was pleased. He was really astute. She'd love to show him her beautiful Persian Mir, the finest variation of a Sarabande that she'd ever encountered, but apparently, it was long gone. Mustn't let Jake see she was aggravated. Not aggravated, outraged! How dare he take her rugs! Simmer down. Control yourself. Don't let on.

She took two deep breaths and continued her show and tell with Mike about her special rugs.

Jake was staring at Doris. She knew! For sure. He could tell. She was playing a game. Damn her games! Slow torture, that's what she had in mind.

Now they were done. Mike thanked them profusely, Jake locked up, and away they went. For the moment the ordeal was over.

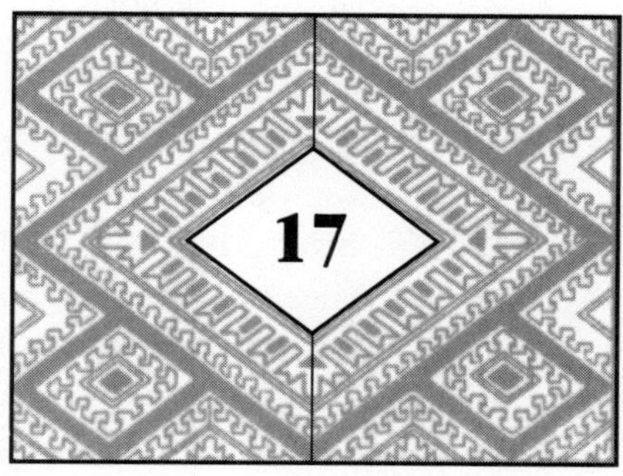

For the record, Rahshi and the other young men working behind the scenes at Classic Design were not immune to the Oriental rug curse that afflicted the rest of the staff. For them it was worse. It was a hands-on experience: carrying the rugs in, carrying the rugs out, unfolding them, refolding them. Close contact.

If raging hormones were the bane and the joy of adolescence, Phil and Gus and Juan and Paulo and so many others down through the years were exposed to an unaccountable acceleration of their already overactive libidos. How did they manage?

They had girl friends. Phil had Donna, Gus had Maria, Juan had Nina. Rahshi had been with Rolanda for almost two years. A store record. A friendly, intimate relationship cost money, lots of it. Expensive gifts, usually of jewelry, were de rigueur. Sophie and Lesley often chided the boys about spending so much on flashy trinkets. They didn't care. The motivation was strong and constant and beyond their control.

Finding a safe haven for their lovemaking was a major effort. They didn't have and couldn't afford cars. In Boston there were few deserted trysting places. They had to plan ahead. They stood guard for each other in their schools (boys' or girls' toilets), in their homes (when no one was about), wherever.

CD was not off limits. More than a few assignations had occurred in the basement storeroom. The boys took turns smuggling in their partners, and on a pile of gorgeous Orientals stacked up for the purpose, they thrilled to the greatest sex of their lives. Despite or because of the risk involved (and certainly because of the rugs), their young women were crazy about doing it at CD. It was a status symbol, screwing at Classic Design.

Jake would kill if he ever found out. Mrs. Seagull would have a full-blown heart attack. Kids befouling her precious Orientals! Lesley and Sophie wouldn't believe that anyone could get past their eagle eyes.

Occasionally one of the girls would brazenly stop by to see her boyfriend. Jake frowned upon such visits. The rest of the crew didn't care one way or another as long as the store wasn't busy. There were awkward introductions and then much whispering and giggling.

A real romance was a problem. It wasn't fair; the potential lovers didn't know what hit them. They had no rug resistance. Poor Paulo. He was in the throes of a passionate affair.

It had started the last December. He was trying to get home to Colombia to attend his sister's wedding. The weather was terrible, cold and wet. A blanket of heavy snow had closed Logan Airport. It was still coming down, but somehow Paulo had managed to get to the airport after work. He should have called. All flights had been canceled. He didn't exactly understand the ground attendant's words or the loudspeaker announcements. His English was not so good, although it was getting better all the time.

There were hundreds, maybe thousands of people stranded that evening. The place looked like a disaster area. All kinds of people hunkering down, trying to get comfortable. Paulo staked out a small patch of floor space with his raincoat and duffel bag. Next to him, a mother and daughter were establishing their territory. They had thought to pack a lunch. The restaurants and snack bars were jammed.

Paulo smiled at the slim, pretty blond girl, the daughter. She smiled back. She had a sandwich in her hand, and with a graceful gesture or two, indicated that she and her mother would share their food with him. She looked appealingly to her mother, who grinned and nodded. Language was not a problem.

They offered him a thick meat sandwich, a chunk of hard cheese, and a pickled green tomato. Paulo ate every crumb. It was delicious. He hadn't realized how hungry he was. He tried to say thank you. A few more gestures. After a bit, he came to understand that they had been in Chicago visiting the mother's brother for the last four weeks. Now they were heading home to Russia. The mother spoke very little English. The daughter had about as much English as Paulo. They understood each other, only the accents were different.

Her name was Tonya. She was seventeen. It was her first big trip, a high school graduation present. She loved America, didn't want to go home. She told Paulo about Chicago. (He hadn't been out of Massachusetts since his arrival in Boston two years before.) With enthusiasm she described some of the places she'd seen: Lake Michigan, Lake Shore Drive, the Magnificent Mile, Water Tower Place, the many skyscrapers. She especially loved the music: jazz, blues, and especially the symphony. Her blue eyes sparkled as the words tumbled over each other.

Paulo was enchanted. They jabbered on together for hours. He told her about the hazards and hardships of living in Colombia. He'd come to the States so he could earn a living. She told him about the new Russia and the changes that were occurring. Everything was getting better.

The mother dozed fitfully.

By sunup, they had established a relationship. More than that, they felt they were in love. Using his duffel as a headrest, they stretched out next to each other. They held hands. They talked and talked. They planned for him to come to Russia the next summer. It all seemed possible.

Now the weary mother roused herself and kept watch.

The morning was bright and sunny. The runways were cleared; air traffic resumed. Paulo's plane was called. There was a tearful embrace, their first. They promised to write and to phone. Tonya walked with him to his gate and, with tears streaming down her cheeks, stood watching his plane taxi out to the field.

That had been six months ago. Paulo, having scrimped and saved on everything except phone calls to Russia, was eagerly anticipating his trip. He was making payments on his ticket. Two months to go.

The rugs didn't make it any easier for him. Being in love in a long-distance relationship and working at CD surely aggravated the hunger. Poor Paulo.

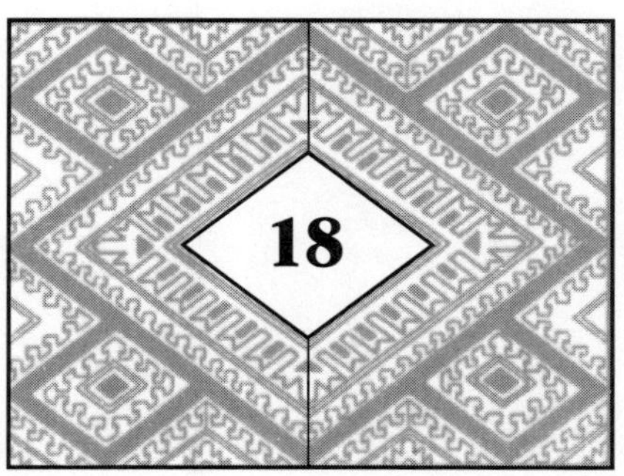

The following Wednesday at Peter's apartment, the two lovers lay abed, a light cotton sheet covering their naked bodies. After an enormously satisfying physical interlude, they were relaxed and chatting amiably. If anything, missing one of their regular rendezvous had added an extra measure of passion to their lovemaking. For the moment their libidos were slaked.

"God, that was good. I missed you so. The time dragged by. Lesley, you have to spend more time with me. How can you stay away?"

"Peter, you know the answer to that. I stay here when I can, when Ken's out of town. If our situations were reversed, could you do any better? How would you explain being away? It's not easy. I'm doing the best I can."

She was thinking: If only I hadn't fallen in love with you, if only we weren't so compatible, if only the sex weren't so great. I didn't even know I was multi-orgasmic until you. No matter what, I can't give you up. She felt a gentle stirring in her groin. Again.

She moved close to Peter. She stretched up to kiss him. Slowly, lovingly, their warm, wet, open mouths and darting tongues signaled the prelude to a second, more leisurely union.

"Such a delightful body," Peter murmured as he cupped her breast and leaned over to lick and suck first one nipple, then the other.

The stirring in Lesley's groin intensified. She stroked his abdomen in a firm circular motion. She reached for his penis. She massaged it gently with her fingertips, then moved down to take it into her mouth, to suck on it, to make it hard and strong.

"That's wonderful. Easy now, let's make it last," breathed Peter.

He pulled her up close to him and hugged her, even as one hand slid over and down her body caressingly, then between her legs and into her very wet vagina. She clung to him as he kneaded her clitoris.

Sensing their mutual need and accord, Peter made it happen. He was atop and into her. They tussled playfully until, their bodies shuddering, they sailed the endless wave to pounding surf.

Afterwards they lay quietly. They were both astounded by their ecstatic explosions. They couldn't get enough of each other.

"I think I'm becoming a sex maniac," said Lesley in a small, troubled voice. "Do you think I am? I keep wanting more."

"Sounds good to me. Count your blessings, darling. We are sensational together. Better and better."

"Peter, I'm not kidding. We're too old for this. We're going to kill ourselves."

"What a way to go! Lesley, you are positively glowing with vitality, and I never felt better."

"Be serious. What if one of us has a heart attack or worse while we're together? What would we do? We should make provisions, find a neutral third person to diffuse any—God forbid—problems. Think about it."

"Okay, but my sons would probably view my remains with awe and pride. I'd be their hero. Sorry, our situations are different. You're right. We need a go-between. I'll give it some thought. It would be a big responsibility. In the meantime, I'm hungry. Let's find something to eat."

They donned their matching terry-cloth robes and scuffs (Peter's thoughtful gift) and headed for the kitchen. Peter put on his latest disc, a new recording of the Ravel Introduction and Allegro. Lesley rummaged through the fridge and came up with an apple, a pear, and a wedge of cheese, which she sliced and arranged on a small wooden platter. Peter opened a bottle of Chianti Classico, grabbed two wineglasses, and led the way into his handsome living room. A beautiful old Herez, newly acquired from CD, graced the parquet floor.

They sat close together on the soft, down-cushioned sofa, sipping the ruby wine and munching on the fruit and cheese. The music cast its spell. The panoramic view of the sun-dappled Charles River was hypnotic. Neither one spoke.

When at last Lesley leaned her head on his shoulder and sighed, Peter took her in his arms and kissed her tenderly, then hungrily. And cradled in the commodious sofa, they made love once again, easily, sensuously. Thoroughly exhausted, they fell sound asleep.

When Lesley opened her eyes, the sun had set. It was twilight. She had to leave, but she couldn't get herself to move. What a perfect afternoon, she thought. She gazed at Peter's handsome, sleeping face. How can I leave him? How, indeed! What about Ken? My husband Ken. We're getting along well these days. He seems happier, more communicative. Am I willing to jeopardize a good, solid marriage? I must be, I'm here. That says something. I'm not up to making decisions. I feel vital and young with Peter. I love him for that. He's a wonderful person. Everything is new and exciting with him.

Deep down Lesley knew that in her fashion she would always love Ken. Life with him was . . . comfortable and companionable. The way it *should* be.

Did she want another life, a very different life? That was the real question. At the moment she was doing double duty, placating and servicing two men. Not too badly either. When she wasn't actively worrying about her precarious predicament, she was savoring every moment of the renascence of her prime. She was, in fact, planning to hold out for as long as she could. Eventually she would have to decide. Not yet. Not just yet . . .

Peter was stirring. Before he opened his eyes, Lesley got up, pulled her robe about her, and headed for the bathroom. He stretched and smiled as he came awake, hearing the water running in the shower. She's here where she belongs. I love her. I love Lesley Kane, married and all! What's to become of us? She'll have to decide. If I press her she'll run away. Patience. That's what I need.

When they'd showered and dressed, they went back to the kitchen to savor a cup of tea together. Their sense of utter fulfillment was almost tangible. Lesley looked at her watch and the spell was broken.

"Ken's in St. Louis. He said he'd call. I've got to get home."

"Tell me you don't want to leave, that you'd rather stay here. Tell me."

"I'd rather stay with you."

"I believe you. Lesley, I'm a patient man. I can wait, but not forever. I need a life. It's up to you."

She nodded. "I know, I know. Don't spoil our day. I feel so happy when I'm with you. Then I remember my . . . real life. I can't tell which is which anymore."

Considering everything, Lesley was becoming more and more aware that her questionable situation suited her fine. She was enjoying the best of two worlds. Someday she'd have to choose. But not today. Some other day.

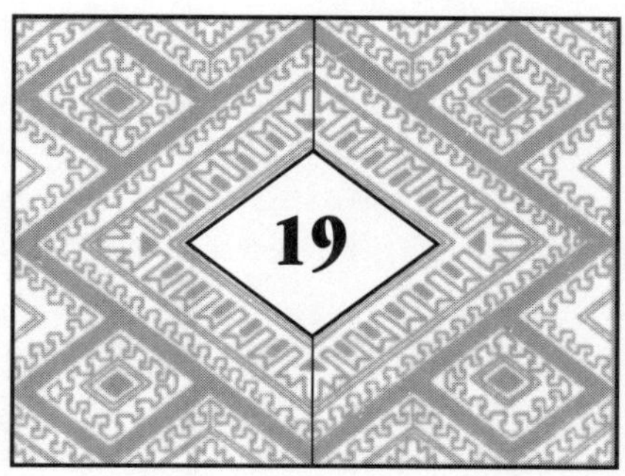

# 19

Ever since Santa Fe, Martin Simon had been sleeping on the couch in his small office just off the master bedroom. It was not comfortable. Unhappily, he was a stickler for a firm mattress and eight hours sleep per night, neither of which he was getting. He was becoming increasingly grumpy and disgruntled. Sarah had the luxury of their king-sized bed, but she was not sleeping well either. When the children wandered in, Martin and Sarah explained away the new sleeping arrangements with a cough or a sneeze, one of them was coming down with a cold or worse, the flu.

They'd talked and talked, saying the same things over and over again. He didn't know, couldn't understand why she was unhappy. He worked hard, made a good living, didn't fool around. She had everything: a beautiful home, three well-behaved children, a decent husband. What was it that she wanted? What was the matter with her?

She couldn't make him understand her disaffection. It had been coming on for a long time, little by little. Nowadays he misinterpreted her devotion to the kids or even a nicely cooked meal as an easing of the tension between them. She told him that she needed to be a person, her own person, not just his wife and mother to Sam and Amy and Lisa. He didn't have any regard for her ideas or opinions. He never even asked her. He was patronizing and domineering. Their life together was one-sided. They did what *he* wanted to do. Their sex life was exactly the same.

Yes, she loved the children, and she was a damn good mother, a better mother than he was a father. She was also a good cook and a pretty fair housekeeper. What difference did that make?

The focus on their relationship was too much. They were at an impasse. Martin refused to talk about sex. He thought professional counseling was a waste of time and money. "It's nobody's business."

They were putting on a happy front for the children. They were also reasonably considerate of each other, but the strain was beginning to tell.

Martin was irritable and jumpy at the office, his bastion of expeditious harmony. He'd yelled at his irreplaceable secretary, sent her home in tears. That was all he needed, to have her quit! Carla had been with him for eight years. Send her flowers, lots of them, immediately!

Not accustomed to the nitty-gritty, which he considered woman's work, he called in a secretary from the steno pool. "Roses for Carla," he told her. "A big bouquet. Don't stint."

His was a fast-paced, dynamic organization. He had to keep all the cogs oiled. What was the matter with him? He knew the answer before the question. It's Sarah. She has me all roiled up. I require peace and quiet at home. My nerves are shot. It's bound to affect my practice. I've got to put an end to her nonsense.

As a person who prided himself in his professional acuity, in knowing every detail of the most complex case, in maintaining his clients' absolute trust, Martin was a veritable giant in the field of law. As a husband and a father, he barely made the grade. What made him an aggressive, successful lawyer didn't translate into a warm, loving family man. He tended to expect the same efficiency, respect, and order at home that he demanded at his office. His word was law. The concept of give and take was beyond him.

That evening as they were getting ready for bed—their separate beds—Martin finally asked the question.

"Sarah, do you want a divorce? Is that what you want?"

He'd never mentioned divorce. She had but then backed off. He thought her a fool. It was a tough, hard world out there alone. She'd be miserable. She had no skills, no real talent. His assessment of her was devastating. He didn't count her beauty or smarts or sensuality. Basically, he knew she was a good person and a caring mother. That was all. In his view, these were not traits valuable in the marketplace.

Sarah said, "I guess it's the only way. We're both unhappy. We deserve better. Admit it."

She watched him closely. What she saw made her furious. He was *pitying* her. For what? For giving up the one and only Martin Simon! He felt sorry for her. He didn't listen, he didn't hear. He'd never understand. He thinks I'm a big zero without him. Nothing. That does it! I'm on my own.

"If you're absolutely certain that's what you want, I'll get the ball rolling. You and the kids will stay here. I'll find a place in town, near the office. We'll talk about community property and child support and custody, all the rotten details. God, Sarah, I can't believe you're serious. What will happen to you? You don't have a profession or special skills. What are you going to do?"

She didn't really know.

"I'll continue working at CD for the time being. I'm seriously considering going back to school. It's about time I pick up a degree or two."

"Listen, Sarah, I don't mind paying for my children's college education, but I have no intention of educating an ex-wife."

"Martin, I will take good care of the kids. How or what I do with the rest of my life is none of your business. I'll get my own lawyer to negotiate with you. That way we can behave like sensible adults and not tear each other to shreds."

Sarah spoke calmly and unemotionally, belying her churning, upset stomach. She was a wreck. Whatever she had to do to earn some measure of respect, she would do. It wasn't going to be easy.

The Simons' marriage was over. No more pretenses. Amy, Lisa, and Sam had to be told, carefully. They had to be made to understand that they were beloved by both parents, and that their mother and their father would always be there for them. Just not under the same roof.

Sometimes people couldn't get along. It happened.

Old story, sad story.

Jake Seagull was waiting for the other shoe to drop. For years he'd been leading a double life. Not even the considerable skills of Mike Hannagan had uncovered the covert activities of the mild-mannered rug merchant. Not yet, anyway. It was no wonder. He'd learned to cover his tracks meticulously. He'd had to.

Ever since he'd married into the family of the infamous Meyer O. Mintz, Jake had trod gingerly, very gingerly. With the family Meyer was a quiet, low-keyed gentleman, but his reputation was so formidable that Jake watched himself very carefully.

The man called Mom was an enigma. His family adored him. He was the patriarch. Doris was his darling. By virtue of his marriage to Doris, Jake was accepted—at least tolerated. But Mom was not crazy about him.

It worked both ways. Jake got the whim-whams whenever he was alone with Meyer. His cold, probing blue eyes belied his benign demeanor. Jake knew his father-in-law would allow no nonsense from him, and he had no intention of giving him cause.

Besides, Jake loved Doris, he really did, in spite of the

obvious negatives. So she was spoiled and demanding, sometimes rude and outspoken. She was also the smartest female he'd ever met, good-looking and interesting to be with. So her nerves were shot. They'd have to take it easy, avoid stress. He would see to it.

And so he did. He smoothed the way for her. He kept her close to him at home and in business. Her money was a big help, no denying it. But Jake earned every dollar Doris shared with him. Meyer could find no fault. Jake toed the line.

When Meyer died, Jake breathed a sigh of relief. Nothing actually changed but Jake's sense of responsibility. He lightened up. He began to think of himself and of all the things he'd suppressed during the years of Mom's intensive surveillance. Doris, of course, was heartbroken, inconsolable. Never again would she find such unconditional devotion, not even from Jake. A husband could never match her father's blind constancy. It was a terrible loss for her.

Unbeknownst to *anyone,* Jake had always loved the ballet, had even wanted to study dance. Considering his modest circumstances and knowing how hard his parents worked to put him through school, he'd never dared venture far afield of the business courses they had urged on him. They would have been shocked if he had turned to dance. Doris would have laughed at him, and Mom would probably have had his legs broken.

Well, Jake was in the clear now. Without telling a soul, he signed up for an afternoon beginner's class at the Boston Center for the Performing Arts in lieu of one of his regular handball sessions.

He had to buy himself the required paraphernalia: tights, soft leather ballet slippers. He kept the stuff hidden in a brown paper bag in the trunk of his car.

On the first day he was assigned a locker to stow his gear. Good! But the laundry problem remained. How would he explain *tights* to Doris? He couldn't. So he wore sweat-dried workout clothes instead.

Jake loved his class. He was one of three men in it, the oldest and the chubbiest. There were seven women. He learned the basic positions, after a fashion. He worked at the barre. He was sore and awkward, but he had heart. His pliés were pitiful, his jetés a joke. Jake laughed loudest. His hopes were high.

His dance teacher was patient. She recognized honest effort. Jake was trying his best. The sad truth was that Jake was a klutz. No amount of class or work could change that. She let him stay in the class until the end of the semester. Then, in a private interview, she suggested tactfully that perhaps tap dancing would be a more suitable means of expression for him.

Jake wasn't too perturbed or deterred. Right away he pictured himself as Gene Kelly in *Singing in the Rain*. He had taps put on his best loafers and signed up for an afternoon course in tap dancing. As far as he could tell, no one was onto him yet.

Jake loved the tap routines. He was a quick study. But his ungainly, off-balance maneuvering sabotaged his dreams. He was asked to leave the class.

Jake was rocked this time. He attributed his dancing fiasco to his age. He was too old to embark on such strenuous activity.

He thought for a long time about his next move. He was an opera buff—everyone knew that. At CD on Saturdays, the radio was always tuned to the Texaco Metropolitan Opera broadcast. Sometimes he sang along, softly, with the tenor. It was great fun. Okay, he would study opera.

He signed up for private lessons at the Boston Conservatory. No more group classes. A wise move. His voice teacher seemed impressed when he auditioned for him. In fact Signore Bendidi was astounded by his performance. He thought Jake was kidding, putting him on.

Jake wasn't kidding; he was doing the best he could. He heard the music perfectly; he read the music adequately. Something happened between the written notes and Jake's inner workings. Whether it was in the diaphragm or the chest or the throat, somewhere the melodic line got fouled. What came out was off-pitch and flat. Maestro Bendidi had to grit his teeth each time Jake let loose. Poor Jake! Poor Bendidi!

The maestro encouraged Jake to practice the basics: single notes and scales, with a piano. And to listen.

Jake didn't have much spare time, and Doris seemed to resent the little time he spent at the piano. She had a better ear than he. Jake's caterwauling got on her nerves. She had no idea that he was *seriously* trying to study opera.

Although Signore Bendidi was a kindly person, he too was having problems with Jake. Once he understood that Jake had no talent, that the lessons were pointless, he worried how to terminate their relationship. His reputation was at stake. His colleagues joshed him about the squawking noise emanating from his studio on Tuesday afternoons. He didn't want to kill Jake's love for opera, but he had his professional standards.

After much deliberation and some astute negotiations, Bendidi came up with an acceptable compromise. The man was a born diplomat.

His dear friend and compatriot, Signora Bertalucci, agreed to take over Jake's operatic coaching. Once a diva in the minor leagues (road show opera companies), the signora was long retired and ever short of funds. She lived in a small, one-bedroom apartment in the North End, the colorful Italian section of Boston. Bendidi kept an eye on her, sending her occasional sustenance in the form of well-heeled, below-par operatic hopefuls. She managed to eke out a living.

When Signore Bendidi first advised Jake that he'd found him the perfect coach, Jake was disappointed. He loved walking the long halls of the conservatory, hearing snatches of vocal and instrumental music echoing from the practice rooms, being part of the music scene. The signore explained he was obliged to give preference to full-time conservatory students, and his schedule was overloaded. He was sorry, but he knew Jake would enjoy working with Signora Bertalucci.

She was expecting a call from him to make arrangements. Bendidi handed Jake a paper with the information, wished him well, and drew a long, deep sigh of relief.

Under the signora's tutelage, Jake had made great strides, at least in repertoire. He visited her once a week on different days to avoid establishing a pattern. He'd become fond of the old prima donna. The cozy recesses of her red-velvet-draped abode, the doorways hung with colored glass beads, the walls papered in flocked arabesque designs, pleased him. The exotic ambiance put him in the mood. He was at his most relaxed with Signora Bertalucci.

In turn she had come to appreciate Jake. The money he paid her was a godsend, and she was a true believer. She praised his efforts extravagantly. A little deaf, she encouraged him to sing out ever more *fortissimo.* She gave him tea and told him stories of her bygone days. If she was in the mood, she'd even vocalize with him. Jake ate it up. The forty dollars a lesson was worth every penny.

Meanwhile, how long before Hannagan got wind of his continuing subterfuge? Jake wasn't sure. He was being extra cautious, but he had the feeling he was walking a tightrope. What with his best customers being robbed, his wife's behavior, and Hannagan's constant snooping, he knew he was living on borrowed time.

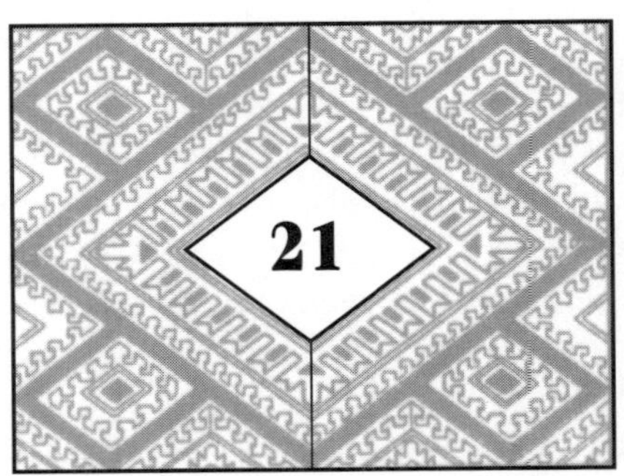

The day had started well at CD.

They were finishing coffee and getting down to business. The front door was open as usual. A well-dressed, familiar-looking black man poked his head in. "Anybody home?" he called. His voice was familiar too. Then, to the crew's amazement and delight, in walked the inimitable Bill Bailey, TV superstar, trailed by his beautiful wife Fernanda. The first customers of the day. They were in Boston, Sophie, the house sleuth, soon learned, to headline a gala benefit for the Children's Hospital, one of the Baileys' favorite causes. They had time to spare. They loved Orientals; here they were. They could use a big, beautiful rug. "Show us."

It was a fun morning. The Baileys were knowledgeable and nice. Their reactions to the various rugs were loud and clear, unmistakable. Everyone got into the act, trying to show off the merchandise. Sophie, being a longtime Bailey fan, was thrilled to have them in the store. That they loved Orientals was an added kick. When they bought one of her favorite Joshaghans, she could hardly contain herself. Imagine the Baileys living with her Joshaghan! The pattern of diamond shapes in a tight grid reminded her somehow of snowflakes.

She'd always found the deep red ground pleasing, so too the design with its light and dark blues accented in ivory. And now the rug had found a home. And what a home! She had to call Jake.

The afternoon was a different story. Nary a person had ventured in. The faithful crew, having completed its chores and exhausted chatter about the Baileys, was talking shop. How to drum up business was the topic.

"Another mailing," suggested Jon halfheartedly.

"What about a sale? We've never had one. I know the Seagulls pride themselves on never having a sale, but with business so slow, why not?" ventured Sarah.

"Mrs. Seagull won't allow it. Doris hates to part with her rugs at top price. It's almost a favor when she lets someone buy one of her babies. She'd never discount one of these rugs. Forget a sale," said Sophie emphatically.

"There must be something we can do. We'll all be out of work if business doesn't pick up. That article in the *Globe* last week about the unsolved mystery of the stolen rugs from CD didn't help. I wonder why Hannagan's dragging his feet? I've got a feeling Mike knows more than he's telling us," Lesley said.

"We don't need the publicity. We were lucky to stay out of the papers for so long." Sophie had expected the story to break weeks ago. She was fairly sure now that Hannagan was onto something, but she wasn't anxious to hear what it was.

"Let's do a sandwich board with a gorgeous Oriental, our name and address, and send Rahshi out to lure in some people. Maybe they'll follow him—Pied Piper effect," kidded Jon. "Or maybe a TV spot with Bill Bailey. Bet that costs a bundle. But that's not our style either."

"Talk, talk, talk. That's all we do. Lesley, may I borrow your newspaper? I haven't seen a paper in days. I'm totally out of touch," said Sarah with a tired sigh.

Martin Simon had moved out of their home in the suburbs. He'd taken a room at a small hotel near his office. His physical leavetaking was more of a wrench than either he or Sarah had anticipated. They were both in shock, and the children were miserable. Not a happy scene.

Sarah sat now at the desk with the *Boston Globe* in front of her. She glanced at the headlines, read a couple of paragraphs, tried to follow the front page story on Bosnia, then bagged it. Her powers of concentration were zero. As was her custom, she flipped pages to the lottery results. A perfunctory once-over, and she moved to the horoscope section. Pisces people were in for a good day. Okay! Not that she put much faith in the stars, still . . . As she followed her children's assorted horoscopes, something clicked in her head. The numbers! What were the numbers? She grabbed her leather shoulder bag from a drawer and fumbled for her wallet. She pulled out a wrinkled white ticket from her billfold, stared at the numbers, then turned back to the lottery page. She read: 3, 5, 25, 32, 40, 49. For the first time in her life, she hadn't played the family birthdays; she'd let the machine do the choosing. Quik Pic, they called it. No wonder she didn't recognize the numbers. Again she checked her ticket against the Megabucks digits: 3, 5, 25, 32, 40, 49.

She handed Sophie the *Globe* and asked her to read back the numbers. Slowly. Sophie did: 3, 5, 25, 32, 40, 49.

"Oh, my God. I've won, I've won," whispered Sarah in awe.

"How much? Do you know how much?" asked Sophie, always the practical one. "Will you have to share the jackpot?"

"I don't know. I don't know. How do I find out?"

"I'll call. Let me think. The lottery headquarters are in Braintree. Hold on."

She got the number from Information, made the call, talked for a minute or two, jotting notes on a scrap of paper. Sarah sat in a daze, watching her.

Sophie hung up the phone. She reached for Sarah, pulled her to her feet, and gave her a big hug.

"It's all yours. You were the only winner. Eleven million dollars! Wow! Couldn't happen to a nicer person or at a better time. Say something, Sarah. You look pale. You're not going to faint, are you?"

"I can't believe it. This happens only in the movies. I don't know anyone who's ever won the lottery," said Sarah weakly. She sat down.

Jon pulled her up and danced her around the store, laughing and singing "Diamonds Are a Girl's Best Friend."

In the midst of the excitement, Mike Hannagan walked into the store. Hearing the news, he swore softly under his breath, and as Jon released Sarah, he swept her into a great big bear hug. It was the first body contact between them. The electricity was startling. He whispered something in her ear and released her quickly. Even in her present giddy state, Sarah sensed that Mike was about to play a major role in her future, which suddenly loomed bright and cheery. Who said money wasn't important?

The phone rang and Lesley picked up. It was Jake. She updated him on the latest, amazing development. He asked to speak to Sarah, congratulated her, and in a semi-serious tone offered to sell her the store. He'd give her a good price. Sarah giggled. Jake wasn't exactly kidding. He told her to take the rest of the day off.

Sarah didn't know what to do with herself. Sophie explained the procedure to her. She had to go to the lottery headquarters in Braintree, about fifteen miles south of Boston, fill out the tax and claim forms, be interviewed, have her picture taken, and that was it, according to the telephone spokesperson. It would take about an hour. She'd receive her first check right there. The payoff would be made over a twenty-year period; the next nineteen payments would fall on the anniversary of the first check. "That's all there is to it. Go get it," urged Sophie.

"I have to call Martin and the kids. No, I don't. But I will. I don't think I can drive there alone. Yes, I can. I sound like a raving lunatic. I have to sit down for another minute. I should make a list. Oh and Lesley, remember that little Persian kilim that I love? Would you take it out of inventory for me? That's going to be my first extravagance."

Mike, who would dearly have loved to take Sarah in hand,

was holding back. This she had to do by herself. It was the start of her new life. She said she wanted to be independent, her own person. What an opportunity! Go for it, woman, it's all yours. I'll see you down the road a piece. If you're agreeable, we're going to make some music together.

Meanwhile downtown, the call from Sarah had unnerved Martin Simon. He did some quick arithmetic in his head and mused over the luck of the draw. He never knew she played the lottery—the act of a desperate person, in his opinion, or a real sucker. Which? But she'd won. Good! At least he wouldn't have to pay alimony. He'd have to pay for the children's education; he wanted to do that. Maybe Sarah could pay half. She was going to have plenty of money. Now he'd be able to afford another life, another wife, even more children. Hell, who was he kidding? He made a good living—a bloody fortune, for that matter. The great thing was that he wouldn't have to worry or feel guilty about poor Sarah. Poor Sarah, indeed!

That afternoon, as Sarah drove slowly and cautiously south to collect her unexpected booty, the first payment, she remembered what Mike had whispered in her ear. "Money or no money, I'm making my move on you. Just tell me when. We're going to ring all the bells." She smiled. Already she felt a longing for him. God, she actually had the hots for him! Thanks to Jon and their custom-made sex courses, 101 and 102, she was in touch with her sensual self. She and Jon, bless him, had been very good for each other. What an incredible day! Bill Bailey in the morning, the lottery in the afternoon. She glanced at her watch. And it was only three o'clock.

For two weeks, Sarah had been having the time of her life! First the money: Martin had all kinds of ideas for the initial check. She listened to him patiently with no intention of following his advice. Sink or swim, she was handling this herself. Then the president of the local bank where she kept a small checking account called to congratulate her and tell her what to do with her new wealth. If anything, he was more patronizing than Martin. She thanked him profusely, telling him she would consider his suggestions. He was taken aback. He went so far as to say that if she didn't do what he said, the money would probably be lost. What nerve!

She did consult with a neighbor whom she knew Martin respected. He was with an investment firm in Boston. He gave her a list of qualified money managers; she chose the only woman on the list, Claire Grasso. Claire was helpful and supportive and agreed that a conservative approach was best: stocks, bonds, and Treasury notes. Claire established an interest-bearing checking account for her, funded with $50,000 of the money. All in all, Sarah felt comfortable with the arrangements. That done, she decided it was time to try her wings.

The children were first on her agenda. She spent a mindless few days making their dreams come true. Her son Sam could now match his sporting equipment with any well-stocked store. Lisa and Amy had whole new wardrobes and their own telephone, and the bedroom they shared was in the process of being redecorated. They'd had such fun deliberating over their choices. Whatever they'd wanted—within reason—she'd okayed.

Not that they were deprived children. Sarah was the one who had grown up in a family that had to watch every penny. It was a habit instilled in her, not in her kids. Martin hated her penny-pinching ways. Her addiction to sales and discount stores exasperated him. Still she'd managed to furnish their home with such love and good taste that no one except Martin realized that it was not filled with priceless antiques and costly accessories. She'd haunted secondhand stores and antique barns until she'd found exactly the right pieces. She'd had chairs repaired and refinished, sofas stripped down, rebuilt, and reupholstered. The house was charming, and Sarah took pride in it. Martin had saved a bundle—not that it mattered anymore.

She was the same way about clothes. She didn't own anything that hadn't been bought off the sale rack. Even so, with her tall, willowy figure, she usually looked like a fashion model (working at CD had improved her style considerably). At one time Martin had been so disgusted with her that he'd sent his secretary out to choose a black lace cocktail dress for Sarah to wear to a particularly important business dinner. He needn't have bothered. Once Sarah became aware of her great body, and that happened early on at Classic Design, she grew more confident in selecting her discount clothes. Perhaps her taste was not to Martin's liking, but Sarah was a knockout in whatever she wore.

She was better with the children. Each fall she outfitted them in the latest fashion in school togs. For the rest of the year, she shopped at Marshall's or T. J. Maxx or wherever she found the best buys. Sam didn't care what he wore. The girls did, and they grew more difficult by the year. They knew to go to their father if they wanted something special. He never said no. But then they were dealing with a man who didn't know or care about sales. He bought his own clothes at Brooks Brothers when he needed them, full price. He enjoyed countermanding Sarah when it came to economy.

Martin Simon should be grateful. He'll never find a second wife as thrifty, thought Sarah. Well, it's my turn. I'm going shopping today. Retail.

Sarah thought wistfully of the Billy Barnes stories. If only Billy were here now. He'd love this. He'd know where to go and what to buy. His taste was fabulous. Poor Billy. All the things he might have done.

Sarah targeted Neiman Marcus at Copley Place for her first solo expedition. A little shy and somewhat reluctant, she parked her car in the garage under the shopping center and headed for the store. At Neiman's she squared her shoulders, asked for designer's clothes, and took the escalator up to the third level. A sales rack caught her attention immediately. She turned over a few price tags and broke into a cold sweat. They couldn't be serious. One dress was marked down to $1,400, another to $2,200. She was in the wrong department.

"May I be of any help?" asked an elegantly dressed, chignoned saleswoman.

"I need some clothes, but these are out of my price range. Do you have a less expensive department?" Right away Sarah was annoyed with herself. She could afford anything she wanted. What the hell was the matter with her?

The woman told her to try the second floor. Down went Sarah, meek as a lamb. This time she ignored the markdown racks and went straight to a salesperson.

"I'd like to put together some separates. Could you help me? I'm a size eight."

The smartly dressed, older woman did a quick study and recognized Sarah's distress. "Cheer up," she said. "Shopping isn't that bad. With your face and figure, you should be having a ball. Let me show you a few things."

Sarah followed the woman, Mrs. Green, according to her name tag, as she moved from one area to another, choosing a Donna Karan skirt here, a Sonia Rykiel jacket there, an Ellen Tracy blouse, Calvin Klein slacks and a sweater, the whole works. Sarah began to relax. She picked up a softly muted mohair sweater by Ralph Lauren and a short, heather tweed skirt to go with it. She spotted a nicely tailored red leather blazer. She'd always wanted a red leather jacket. Beginning to enjoy herself, Sarah gathered an armload of clothes as she trailed her salesperson. She had never not looked at prices before.

"Why don't you start by trying on these things? If they fit, and if you like them, I'll bring in more." The pleasant Mrs. Green ushered her into a spacious fitting room.

As Sarah tried on one outfit after another in the mix-and-match assemblage, she was more than pleased with her mirror image. In fact she could hardly believe that the reflection in the glass was really Sarah Simon. Each new change was more becoming than the last. She smiled at herself. How to choose? She couldn't have everything. Who *said*? She waged a little war with herself.

Mrs. Green returned with another load of colorful separates. She nodded approvingly as Sarah modeled a vivid yellow and black Escada skirt and jacket.

"It's perfect. You look like a page from *Vogue*. I don't know how you can eliminate a thing. I'm going out to find you a wonderful coat. That's what's missing."

Sarah tried on the rest of the clothes. That she could mix one thing with another and another tickled her. She'd have an infinite variety in her closet. What fun! She decided to take everything. When Mrs. Green returned with a long, loose black ulster coat, she grinned delightedly.

"It's exactly right. It will go over everything. I love it. Thank you."

Mrs. Green was astonished when Sarah announced she

would take the lot and that she would wear the black skirt and blouse and the red leather blazer.

"Are you sure? Let me write up the sales slip, and you can check off each item. You may want to change your mind."

"I'll be in the shoe department while you're wrapping my clothes. Maybe you can put them on hangers? How will I ever get them home?"

"Don't worry. If you're sure you want them all, I'll have them delivered to your car. Just tell me where and when."

Money smooths the way, observed Sarah wryly.

Mrs. Green handed her the itemized slip. Sarah had to sit down. Do it, she said to herself, write the check. Her happy salesperson stood over her, beaming encouragement.

Buying shoes was easier. Basic colors and styles plus two trendy pairs of high fashion boots, all of the softest, most supple leather. She wrote another huge check. Now she had to go home and lie down. She was feeling slightly ill.

She was thinking of the assorted appeals for money from so many organizations and private, suffering people. She didn't know what to do. Some of the cases were clearly fraudulent; most were not. She'd asked Claire Grasso to help her sort through the requests. Considering that her money was a fluke to start, she felt obliged to share some of it with the less fortunate.

There was another project she had in mind. As soon as she returned to work, she'd get the ball rolling on it. She had to talk to Jon.

Even though it was a school night, she decided to take the children out for supper. They'd settle into a regular routine once she got the hang of this new lifestyle. She'd better get back to work. That should sober her up.

At work the following Monday, Sarah was greeted as a conquering hero. After coffee and scones for all, her treat, she was pelted with questions about her winnings. She answered as best she could, still not very sure of herself.

"How long have you been playing the lottery? Did you always play the same numbers? Where did you buy the lucky ticket?" Jon was incredulous.

"I've been buying a two-dollar Megabucks ticket every week for years. At the liquor store on the next block. The funny thing is that this time, this one time, I took a Quik Pic instead of my usual numbers. You know the usual numbers are my family's individual birthdates. Who would believe it?"

"You won on a Quik Pic? You didn't even choose your own numbers! Aren't we ridiculous, sweating over numbers?" The unflappable Sophie laughed. Like the rest of her cohorts, Sophie had been bitten by the lottery bug. She'd been investing daily. They all had.

"Wait a minute. I bought one, only one ticket per week, not per day. Don't think about it or talk about it. If it happens, it's a bloody miracle. I'm the living proof. Don't count on it; it's too crazy." Sarah cautioned them about wasting their hard-earned cash on a dream. But they faced the same odds as she had. Why should she discourage them? A dream was important. She vowed to keep her mouth shut.

A lone customer wandered in. She asked to see their Turkish kilims. Jon and Sarah rose to the challenge. There was a big pile of kilims at the back of the store. Flatwoven Oriental rugs were popular in contemporary settings. Their one drawback was their very narrow width. Usually woven by nomadic people in tents, the rugs' width was limited of necessity, not so the length.

With a flourish Jon threw open two or three bold, geometric rugs. As expected, the customer loved the rug but complained about the awkward dimensions. Although Sarah explained to the woman that there were none wider, she insisted upon viewing every single kilim in the stack. It was a fruitless search but a good review for Sarah and Jon, seeing the entire kilim inventory anew.

Sarah suggested a Pakistani Bokhara to the skeptical customer. She showed her one. The woman was pleased. It was exactly what she wanted. Jon located the proper size for her, and it was a sale.

After the money transaction was completed, Sarah took Jon to the back of the store again. "I want to talk to you in private. I've been thinking about something you once told me."

"You can't believe a word I say," smiled Jon.

"Be serious. Remember you asked me what I would do given the opportunity and the money to do anything I pleased. You said you'd open an antique store, didn't you?"

"I guess I did. It's a pipe dream, that's all. Helps me get through my dreary days."

"It doesn't have to be a pipe dream, Jon. We can do it together. I'll be your silent partner. I'll put up the money or arrange the financing. You find the location. And think of a name. If you still want to, we'll go into business." Sarah beamed as she watched Jon's reaction.

He couldn't believe his ears. "Do you mean it?"

"I do, I do," laughed Sarah. "Nothing would make me happier. You'll have your own shop on your own terms. You'll have to do some scurrying, but with your astute eye and your uncanny ability to discover great stuff plus my lottery money, we'll make it happen."

"Sarah, I love you. You're the best. It'll be strictly business," he added hastily. Their sex romps were over; circumstances had changed. He and Nedra and Heidi were back on track. They were spending quality time together and enjoying it. Now he was being given a chance to start his own business, a dream come true. He couldn't ask for more. "I've never had a better friend, Sarah. I'll get on it PDQ. You won't be sorry."

"I know it, and I feel the same way about you. But let's not get mushy. Don't give notice at CD until we see how soon we can get organized. And let's not talk here."

Just thinking of Jon as an entrepreneur in the world of antiques put Sarah in a great mood. This is more like it, she thought to herself.

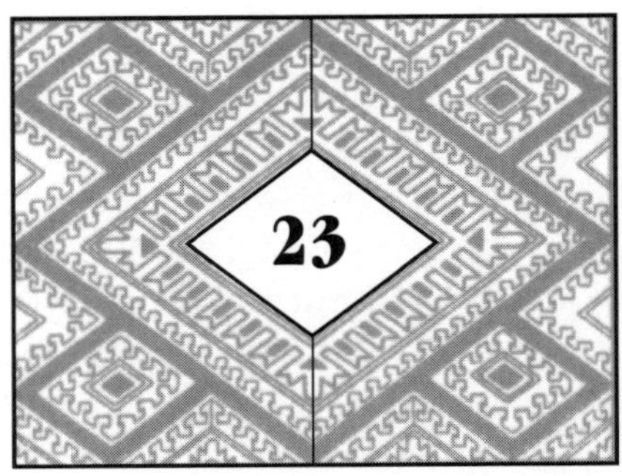

What was it with Mike Hannagan? He was dragging his feet. Why? He knew who was responsible for the rug thefts and where the rugs were stashed. There was only one hitch. He didn't know who had actually ripped off the rugs, who broke into the eight houses and carried off the heavy booty. He needed to interrogate the brains behind the operation, to lean on the culprit. So?

Day after day he worked on the rest of his case load with reasonable success. There was more than enough bloodshed, rape, armed robbery, and drug trafficking in Boston to keep the whole police force busy. He wasn't sure why he was so reluctant to act on this particular case: something about the store, about the people, about the rugs.

His obsession with Sarah was another matter. He'd been so damned randy of late that he'd actually taken to whacking off when he lay abed thinking of her. Hadn't done that since he was a kid. No need. He'd always had available, obliging female partners whenever he got the urge. Since his divorce five years ago, there'd been no shortage of lady friends, much to his surprise.

He was no great shakes as a husband. Lord knows Annie

told him that often enough. They had both mistaken physical attraction for real love. They'd been such dumb kids. Once their great appetites were appeased, and it had taken a while, they didn't have much in common. They didn't care enough about one another. The marriage foundered. There were recriminations, a terrible loss of self-esteem, and finally, a lousy divorce. They had both learned a hard lesson.

Now here he was again, letching after another beautiful woman. He admired Sarah's determination to stand alone. She thought she didn't need anyone to take care of her. Hell, she had three children to look after; she was no kid! Mike was enthralled, but . . . liberated women had never appealed to him before. He'd considered her a fool, leaving a cushy home and a decent man. He could see she was miserable, but in this cold, mean world, what were her chances? Mike had seen the alternatives. She'd be better off staying put.

That was yesterday. Today he wasn't so sure. She'd hit the jackpot! Big! She could do as she pleased, afford options, security. The money would pave the way. She said the money was a bonus, not the determining factor. But that was because she didn't know about hardship conditions.

Like Martin Simon, Hannagan breathed a sigh of relief. Though it was none of his business, he too had been worrying about Sarah. What was she to do? How was she to live? A lot better than a lean and hungry, not to mention horny, Boston shamus, he thought to himself. Get on with it!

His quandary over the rugs was a first for Mike, who prided himself on cool, objective work habits. Sooner or later he'd have to call it a wrap. It was time to ace the getaway truck. There was a dark green, unmarked panel truck seen in the vicinity of four out of the eight thefts. Apparently unobtrusive, it had taken some serious prompting to conjure up a picture of any truck in the minds of the residents who lived nearby. He'd made the rounds of numerous trucking companies, a thankless, time-consuming task. He'd narrowed the possibilities, but he knew he was still whistling "Dixie." If the shortest distance between two points, A and B, was a straight line, why didn't he go to point A? Why indeed?

Actually Mike was closer than he knew. That very afternoon when questioning the dispatcher at G & L Transportation, the panel truck, gleaming from a fresh coat of red paint and newly applied bold, black lettering on either side, was sitting in the yard, not twenty feet from where he'd parked his old Chevy. Nothing seemed amiss at G & L, no unmarked green trucks in the garage or on the premises.

But as soon as Mike left, the dispatcher called his boss to advise him that a plainclothes cop had been snooping around. He was told not to worry, probably just routine. The message, however, did not sit well with the headman.

It must be Benny. What's he up to? I knew Dad was going to get us in trouble. It was just a matter of time. It's a different world. No, I'm being ridiculous. He's eighty-two years old; he's not in the rackets anymore. I sound like an idiot! We've got a legitimate operation here, by the book. What's the matter with me?

Mark Bloom, a forty-two-year-old man of medium height, weight, and coloring, was clearly agitated. He'd worked hard to make G & L a success in spite of his father, who still thought himself the kingpin. He dearly loved old Benny Bloom even though he'd spent his entire life rebelling against him. Their standards were very different. No one could believe that drab, hardworking Mark Bloom was the only son and heir of the genial, flamboyant Benny Bloom, whose notorious past was best left buried, undisturbed.

Mark knew his father too well. The man was so downright good-hearted and good-humored that he could con anyone into doing his bidding, no matter how outrageous. Benny had been legit for years. G & L, for Getting Legal, was his little joke. Only Mark was aware of the small touches of larceny that his sweet father still tried to perpetrate. Benny was an original. Nowadays he regarded himself a philanthropist, a pillar of society, the mainstay of his synagogue, an admirable person. That was his opinion.

Was there a relationship between Benny Bloom and Classic Design? The man was certainly no connoisseur of Oriental rugs. Regardless, the affable old man was the missing piece in Hannagan's puzzle. Doris Seagull and Benny Bloom were well acquainted. Once Mike made the connection, the jig would be up.

# 24

Sarah and Jon, on a break from CD, were sitting at a table at the Coffee Connection. Sipping coffee and munching on biscotti, they were engrossed in naming their business venture.

"Traditions. What do you think of that? Antiques and collectibles. Sarah, do you like the name Traditions?"

"Hmm, sounds good. Let me think about it."

"I've gone through the junk in my cellar, and I've got boxes of stuff. I knew haunting the flea markets would pay off one day. Now we need some real antiques, important things."

Jon was determined to come up with the perfect name. "How about Best of Times or The Way We Were? What about Estate Finds or Attic Treasures?"

"Don't try so hard. I hate cutesy. Keep it simple. Traditions is okay. Jon, shouldn't we carry a few old rugs? We're both knowledgeable. It would be fun. If Jake is willing to deal with us on commission or wholesale, it'll be a piece of cake. If not, we'll find them ourselves. We know enough resource people. What do you say?"

"I don't know, Sarah. Jake's been a pain in the butt

recently. Haven't you noticed? He'll have a bird when the two of us quit."

"Not the two of us, just you. I'm your silent partner, remember. Nobody except Nedra is to know. I'll stay at CD while I decide what I want to do. I think I'm going back to school, to pick up my undergraduate degree, at least."

"Now that you mention it, Jake has been a little strange. The other day, I swear he was talking to the old Afshar Oriental in the back. We all talk to ourselves now and then, but this was different. He looked embarrassed when I kidded him. He stuttered something, grabbed his jacket, and stormed out of the store."

Jake had been a nervous wreck since the day at the warehouse when Doris showed Mike Hannagan her private collection or what was left of it. He respected his wife's keen rug eye. There was no way in this world that she hadn't noticed the serious gaps in her hoard, the rugs that he'd appropriated and sold off at CD. She didn't say a word then; she still hadn't. She'd been as sweet as sugar candy, more agreeable than he could remember. But Jake knew . . . she was going to put it to him. But when? The suspense was making him crazy. Which, he suspected, was the idea.

She was calm, considerate at home, polite and pleasant with the few customers that stopped by the store, and positively amiable with the bewildered staff. (They weren't used to it.) Jake was the bundle of nerves. He'd already canceled two sessions with Signora Bertalucci. He was finding no solace in his music these days. Even in the shower he could hardly croak a simple scale.

On one score, though, Jake could rest easy. Hannagan knew all about his voice lessons with the signora. His subterfuges amused the detective, who was sympathetic to Jake. Hell, the man was entitled to a harmless pastime. If trying to sing opera made him happy, so be it. Mike had no intention of divulging his secret. It was a sad day when a person had to go to such lengths to cover up a harmless diversion. Mike wondered about the Seagulls' relationship . . .

And at the Coffee Connection, Sarah and Jon, having drained their cups, were getting ready to leave.

"I love the idea of rugs. They'll have to be small ones, though, nothing larger than four by six. There won't be enough space. Sarah, will you look at two locations this weekend? Nedra is excited about one of them." Jon was so full of enthusiasm, he couldn't stop smiling.

"If Martin takes the children, no problem. If not, I'll have them, and I warn you they have short attention spans. Between their father leaving home, and their mother winning the lottery, they don't know which way is up."

"I'd say it's all up," laughed Jon as he and Sarah shrugged on their jackets and headed for CD. She grinned happily at him.

◆ ◆ ◆

Sophie welcomed them back. The store was deserted; there were no customers in sight. Sophie, a remarkably intuitive woman, had noticed a subtle change between Sarah and Jon. They appeared to be closer than ever, but the sexual tension was missing. Something had happened. Was it the money? The rugs still cast their spell, Sophie was convinced. Sarah was not immune. Sooner or later her affected libido would out. She needed a man.

Lesley, usually absorbed in her own complicated life, made the same observation. Money was okay, but an active, satisfying sex life made you feel good, made you pretty. Sex was vital. Sarah would have to take a lover or two. Discreetly, of course.

How did Sarah feel about sex now? The same. Martin was gone. No more brief, well-mannered weekly copulating. She was in her prime. The Persian rug voodoo couldn't be denied, though some might scoff at it. At night in her empty king-sized bed, she found temporary relief in masturbating. At least it put her to sleep. She knew she needed a partner, but a woman in her position had to be careful. And what position was that? she asked herself.

She always waited till she was safely abed to think of Mike Hannagan. As she pictured him, her hand slipped between her legs into the wetness. She remembered his quick hug and the feel of his hard body against hers the day she won the lottery. At the thought, her moist vaginal lips contracted around her slim fingers. She found the key to her sexual release, fiddled with the lock, and rocked into a brief but comforting orgasm. Was this any way for a normal, healthy woman to behave? she wondered as she drifted into a dreamless slumber.

The more Sarah and Mike fantasized in private about each other, the more stilted and formal their actual encounters. They'd gone from casually friendly to self-consciously aware. Today was no exception. CD, at least, provided a cover.

As Mike and Sophie carried on their easy bantering, Sarah studied the man who stirred her so. No one would ever call him handsome—attractive, yes, in his lean, craggy maleness. His steely blue eyes seemed to penetrate all they surveyed. Damn! She felt herself becoming damp at the explicit thought of his cock filling her. She blushed furiously, praying nobody would notice. She tried to think of something else, anything: the new rug, the Azeri that had just arrived. It had a windmill and a kangaroo on it. From eastern Turkey? The folk rugs were wild.

At the same instant, Mike glanced over at Sarah. Instead of seeing her in her form-fitting black tunic worn over skinny black pants tucked into high suede boots, he saw a totally nude Sarah smiling at him, glorious in her nakedness. He stared, then blinked. I'm losing it, he thought. Hell, I've lost it.

Lesley, watching them, sized up the situation. From experience. The mating dance. What were they waiting for? She wondered if she should talk to Sarah. It was none of her business, but ah, she knew the pleasure of allowing one's body total fulfillment. Sarah had been looking so peaked lately, even with winning all that money. She needed a lover, and why not Mike? It seemed a perfect fit.

Sophie too, though not nearly as perceptive as Lesley in this case, couldn't help noticing Sarah's and Mike's obvious discomfort. They needed privacy. Should she say something to Sarah? What was the harm? Her marriage was over. Mike was a nice man. Was he suitable for Sarah? What exactly did *that* mean? Don't be a snob.

"Sarah, honey, would you mind getting me some coffee and a chocolate biscotti at the Coffee Connection? I'm having a caffeine attack. I'd go myself, but I'm waiting for a call from UPS." Sophie playing Cupid.

"If you're going, would you get me a small cappuccino with cinnamon?" asked Lesley.

"I'd love a large black coffee and a corn muffin," put in Jon, "if you don't mind."

"No problem. I'd better write it down. Anything else?"

Hannagan offered to tag along and help bring back the goodies. Sarah said nothing. Out they went.

They walked in silence side by side. One block, two. Mike stopped in front of the coffee shop and looked at her.

"I hope I'm not out of line, Sarah, but if I don't get my arms around you soon and feel your body against mine, I'm going to be in serious trouble. I'm not a kid. If I sound ridiculous, it's only because I don't know how to deal with you."

Sarah laughed. "I feel the same way. I'm practically in heat when I look at you. Something has to be done. Are you free this weekend? Martin will have the kids. Come to my house. I'll cook you dinner and then . . ."

"No way. I'm taking you out for a good meal, and we'll see how that goes," said Mike, not trusting himself or Sarah. He was in unfamiliar territory and proceeding with caution.

Sarah recognized his dilemma and felt an enormous rush of empathy, or thanksgiving, or something not easy to define. Never mind. She accepted his invitation.

Now the temptingly rich aroma of coffee lured them into the shop. Standing in line, waiting for the order, Mike and Sarah eyed each other. The anticipating and improvising were almost at an end. Sarah smiled weakly at Mike, who countered with a broad wink. She laughed. All was well.

The rest of the week dragged by for the potential lovers. With never a respite in crime in Boston, Mike was on the go. Sarah kept busy with her job and her children, who seemed relatively normal at the moment. She also spent an inordinate amount of time considering the assorted appeals for money that kept on coming. It was, she felt, her obligation.

Saturday dawned cool and bright. Sarah dressed carefully in the black and yellow Escada suit. She took one look in the mirror and stripped it off. Not right. Today was the day for the lush Ralph Lauren mohair sweater and miniskirt. And the russet suede boots. Not bad, she thought as she surveyed her reflection. Now to get through the day. She was meeting Mike at 6:00 P.M.

For the life of her, Sarah could not remember that workday. She did have total recall of every minute with Mike. They met at Jimmy's, a wonderful, old Boston landmark, famous for its seafood and its picturesque location on the harbor. They had one drink apiece and a couple of complimentary hors d'oeuvres while waiting for their reservation to be called. Mike had a scotch, she had a white wine spritzer. Once seated at their table, Mike ordered finnan haddie; Sarah, mustard-grilled bluefish with boiled new potatoes. He urged her to order the lobster. She passed. She wasn't up to cracking claws and making a big mess. She wanted to concentrate on Mike.

He'd kissed her on the cheek when he'd greeted her. He'd

arrived early and was waiting. Her carefully chosen outfit solicited a long, approving once-over. She told him about the shopping spree after the lottery. As he took her arm, she felt a tingle run through her, settling in her groin. Embarrassing and not easy to ignore.

As they chatted through the meal, the stirring intensified. She thought of the feasting sequence in *Tom Jones* and almost laughed out loud.

"What's so funny?" asked Mike.

She told him. He grinned. He knew the scene. His twinkling blue eyes were too much for Sarah.

"Let's skip dessert. I've had enough," she said feeling near-faint with desire.

"You have to try the rice pudding. It's the best. Sarah, look at me. I feel exactly as you do. It's okay. We can handle it. Relax."

He was so reassuring that she managed to enjoy dessert, even coffee. He eyed her appreciatively, savoring every word she said, every expression that flickered over her beautiful face, knowing full well that the playacting was over. They were in accord. Nice and easy did it.

Once outside the restaurant, he put his arm around her waist, drawing her close as they walked to his car.

"Your place or mine?" he asked.

"I was thinking mine, but which is closer? I . . ."

He laughed. "You'll be okay, I promise."

In the car, he pulled her quickly into his arms and kissed her firmly, his searching tongue at long last tasting the sweetness of Sarah. She opened her mouth to him, clinging to him, her whole body trembling. After a minute or two he pushed her away and started the car.

"Darling Sarah, we can't do it here. Hold my arm. Tight. We'll go to my place. It's five minutes."

The South End was home to Mike. He had a small, neat apartment in an imposing old stone house also overlooking the harbor. She barely noticed her surroundings. Mike slammed the door behind them, and they were finally alone.

He unbuttoned her coat, then slipped her soft, fluffy sweater over her head in one deft motion. Mike let out an astonished low whistle as he discovered Sarah naked from the waist up.

"What happened to your bra?"

Sarah laughed in spite of herself. It broke the tension. "You're the detective."

They kissed, their mouths hungrily seeking, exploring. Mike cupped one firm, bare breast as Sarah arched her back to him. His breath quickened as his fingertips found and fondled her plump nipple. He shrugged out of his tweed sport jacket, letting it fall in a heap to the floor. With barely a pause, his turtleneck sweater was up and over his head. Sarah gasped at the feel of him.

Her full breasts grazing his hard chest, her face buried in his salty neck, she fumbled to free herself of her remaining clothing. There. It was Mike's turn to gasp. Sarah in the buff was a sight to behold! He nudged her, pushed her urgently toward the big, brown corduroy sofa in front of the fireplace. He stopped momentarily to strip off the rest of his clothes. Sarah watched him slip a condom over his long, thick, rearing penis. "Hurry up."

In his persistent wet dreams, there was much foreplay. Now there was no time. He was on her, his hard shaft against her groin. She opened her legs to him, and he plunged into her warm, wet sex. She lifted up and wrapped her long legs around his waist to achieve the ultimate penetration. Her vaginal muscles contracted, and Mike felt the most intimate, welcoming embrace of his life. And again. He steeled himself to hold. Not possible. Almost against his will, he shuddered, pulling, dragging Sarah into the fierce rhythm of his orgasm. She accepted with pleasure, riding him hard, until she burst into her own spasms.

Panting, they looked at each other with delight.

"Doesn't get much better than that," drawled Mike.

"Great first fuck," agreed Sarah. "Let's get down to business."

Mike had never known anybody like Sarah. The regal bearing, the earthy language, the lusty appetite. What a woman!

"We need more room." He rolled off of Sarah, peeling his condom into a tissue. He picked her up and carried her into his immaculate bedroom, all the while blessing his landlady who cleaned up for him every Saturday. The room was spartanly appointed: a pine double bed, dresser, desk and chair. The furniture was serviceable, neither old nor new. The walls were white and unadorned. The carpet, beige. Only a silky cocoa and white windowpane, plaid comforter softened the monklike atmosphere.

Plopping Sarah onto the bed, he gazed down at her bare-assed beauty and was overcome once again by the need to possess her, to embed himself within her. Sarah, watching him, was hardly a passive participant.

"What do you have in mind, Detective Mike? I note by your dick that something's up." She giggled.

Mike stretched out next to her, thinking about the unfair advantage that women had with their equipment tucked up and away so neatly. "Good of you to notice." He slipped an arm under her shoulder and pulled her on top of him. The feel of her full length against him was intoxicating. He ran his hands over her sides, over her firm butt. He kissed her mouth.

"You're stabbing me," whispered Sarah. She adjusted her position, spreading her thighs enough to grasp hold of his hard penis.

"Careful, lady," said Mike with alarm.

"Don't worry, I have the greatest respect for nature's gifts. God, you're big." She let go, but reached down with one hand to caress and stroke his genitalia.

Mike held still for Sarah's ministrations. He knew he had staying power the second time around. His tongue and fingers tasted and explored her deliciously accessible parts. They both sighed with pleasure. There was no hurry. Mike moved her off him and sat up. He wanted to look at her: the face and shoulders, the firm breasts, her slim waist and narrow hips, the inviting mound, and her long, shapely legs. Watching him,

Sarah felt deeply moved by his long and unabashed gaze of approval.

He touched her nipples gently, then leaned down to suck. She held his head at her breast, running her fingers through his straight, thick hair. He couldn't get enough of her. She loved the insistent tugging of his mouth, wetting her, engulfing one breast then the other. Soon the irresistible sucking created a stirring distinctly not maternal. Mike sensed it. He moved down on her, kissing and licking all the nooks and crannies on the way. With his fingers he opened her gently, probing into the warm, wet folds till he touched her clit. His mouth and tongue took over. Sarah moaned. He stopped momentarily. She breathed easier. Now his tongue was strong and demanding. Sarah was literally purring with pleasure. Mike would have dearly loved to drink in her very essence, to make her come in his mouth, but decided to table that treat for another time. He knelt and reached for a condom. Sarah whimpered for him. He thrust into her; she lifted herself up to receive him, and in an exquisite frenzy, they achieved mutual orgasm.

"Wow, that's what I call fucking!" All of her adult life Sarah had longed for this kind of sex, no-nonsense, straightforward, and completely satisfying.

Detaching and catching his breath, Mike thought to himself, she is a miracle. Propped up on one elbow, he pulled the quilt over their naked bodies. "It's naptime if we're to last the night." That said, he put his head down on the pillow next to hers and promptly fell asleep. He was the master of the quick, refreshing nap.

Sometime later he was awakened by a licking and lapping on his penis. "What the . . ." Sarah was down on him, playing, treating his cock like a double-dip ice cream cone. "Yum," she said.

"You've got a big mouth," he spluttered as she worked his balls. He lay still. She gave as good as she got. What a woman. Everything to please him.

Not exactly.

Sarah was acting out one of her sexual fantasies. Mike was the perfect partner. For starters, she trusted him. Right or wrong, she thought of him as safe and tough, a no-holds-barred kind of man. And she was on the mark.

Mike Hannagan, on the other hand, was getting a tad sloppy. He was thinking with his heart, and he couldn't believe his good fortune. A classy woman like Sarah, worth millions, here in his bed, fucking him, loving him. Detective Hannagan was in trouble. He couldn't help himself. It was a clear case of role reversal.

"Do you like this, that?"

"Don't stop. Am I dreaming? Try that spot again."

Sarah was becoming aroused. Her breathing betrayed her.

"Get up here," Mike commanded.

Sarah did as she was told. They lay on their sides, facing each other. Mike wet his fingers in his mouth, then traced circles around the areole of each nipple. It felt so good that Sarah, watching carefully, did the same to him. He smiled.

"Put your leg up over my hip," he directed her.

Sarah was open to him. They remained in that position for a very long time. Relaxed and unhurried, they pleasured one another with intimate, measured caresses. They kissed long and deep. It was a learning process in slow motion. With one hand Mike guided his hard, swollen penis ever so gently into Sarah, who was moist and inviting. She held her breath as he pressed in as far as he could go. She was aquiver, his balls against her vulva. Willing herself not to move, she concentrated on this new sensation. Mike quickened inside of her. Her vaginal muscles contracted and grasped his cock. Once, twice, again. Control gone, Mike slid into high. Sarah stayed with him.

"Hush, don't say a word. Just hold me." Tears streamed down Sarah's cheeks.

Mike too was deeply moved. They were attuned. Each climax brought ecstatic physical relief, and joy. How was it possible so soon? They fell asleep in each other's arms.

It was a long, wondrous night. The lovers slept in fits and

starts. Awake they reveled voluptuously, their bodies demanding or responding. Their lust seemed endless.

It was almost noon when they awoke the next day. Sarah stretched luxuriously and smiled. Mike was already awake. It was wonderful to see her waking up for the first time in his bed.

"Sarah, I'm plain nuts about you. I've never had such a night. We're made for each other." He hugged her.

"You're absolutely right. I've dreamed of sex like this, and you made it happen. You're wonderful, Mike. I'm so sore and I *still* want more. Can we do this again soon, or do I have to wait for you to ask for another date?"

"Let's take a hot shower and get out of here. We need food. If we eat here, I'm taking you back to bed. They'll find us screwed together, O.D.'ed on sex. How would that look?"

"Not too shabby," deadpanned Sarah.

An hour later at a little restaurant in the neighborhood, they were seated across from one another in a cozy wooden booth. They were ravenous. They'd consumed two plates of scrambled eggs, a heap of hash brown potatoes, and toast, not to mention cups and cups of scalding coffee.

"I'm still hungry," admitted Sarah. "Could we share something else?"

"What an appetite! Where do you put it? Most women I know would rather starve than put on an extra ounce. Not you. I like that. I like *you,* and that's putting it mildly. How about a cheese danish?

"I was thinking more like real food. Would you share a stack of pancakes with me?"

"Sure, if you can eat flapjacks, so can I." Mike reached for her hand. Still luxuriating in a physical glow, they gazed at each other happily.

"Sarah, you are a beautiful woman."

"Thank you, sir. You're not too bad yourself. Has anyone ever told you that you're the spitting image of a young Clint Eastwood?"

"Nope. But after last night, in the eyes of the beholder, anything's possible. Are you busy tomorrow?"

"I'm at Classic Design until five. It's a school night, so I should be home with the kids. I've thought of hiring a housekeeper, but I don't know if that's such a good idea. One of these days I'll get my act together. You'll have to meet my family, Mike. You'll like them."

"If they're yours, I know I will. I have a hunger for you, Sarah."

"And I for you. I don't need coaxing, Mike. No games. We'll figure it out."

They held hands across the table until the platter of pancakes arrived, which they attacked with gusto. There was a sure promise of things to come.

Doris Seagull was home alone, which was not her style. She liked to keep herself programmed. It was a bad day. Clearly agitated, she was pacing the floor. The benign, sweet-tempered façade that she'd adopted of late was gone. She'd been seriously considering her problem, which was out of control. She didn't have a clue about what to do. Damn Jake! He was the thief, the thief who stole her rugs. He knew what they meant to her. How could he? And then to let her bring the detective to the warehouse, with half her collection gone! What was he thinking?

It had been a terrible shock the first time Doris recognized one of her precious rugs at a client's home. It was at the Potters. She and Jake had agreed to stop by to advise them on a rug for their dining room. They loved the old Tabriz they'd found at CD two years before. They were looking for another. Doris had nearly cried when she realized the Tabriz was hers, one of her very first acquisitions. She really adored that old rug. She'd found it at a rug auction; it was love at first sight. She'd had to pay more than she was comfortable with, but it had turned out to be a great buy. It was worth a fortune now. She wondered what the Potters had paid.

She'd managed to keep her cool at the Potters'.

The following week she and Jake were on a similar mission at the Hutchinses' impressive Brookline estate, when she discovered her priceless palm tree Bakhtiari gracing the floor of their handsome paneled library. She'd faked a coughing fit to cover her outrage. They'd had her sit down and sip slowly from a glass of water. With her gorgeous Bakhtiari staring up at her!

That extraordinary rug she'd found at a grungy old secondhand furniture store in Nashua, New Hampshire. She'd spotted it in a corner of the window, rolled up with filthy edges exposed. It was waiting for her. Jake had thought her mad, refused to go into the store. It didn't matter. Once she saw the rug unfurled, she knew. It looked faded and worn, but she knew. The price was ridiculously low; the shopkeeper was happy to get rid of it. He took her money, dumped the rug into a green plastic garbage bag, and carried it out to her car. Jake just shook his head.

Armand, the rug cleaning wizard of Boston, had to put it through four washes before he was satisfied. When he called Doris to come see his handiwork, she was thrilled. The silken sheen of the garden carpet was abloom with glorious, leafy palm trees, all in lovely, mellow colors. It was a beauty. Jake was astounded. He said he'd never doubt her again, that no one had her eye for rugs.

So what *happened*?

She took her rug collecting seriously. Jake *knew* that. When she wasn't buying for the store (Jake acknowledged her superior aesthetic taste and deferred to it), she kept her eyes open for the unusual, the wonderfully rare deviation for herself. Technically, the store paid for the rugs, but they were hers. Jake kept score and handled the financial end. She'd trusted him. A mistake! Daddy was right. He'd never wanted her to marry Jake. If Daddy were here now, he'd know what to do, how to get her out of this mess.

"I really miss you, Daddy," she whispered aloud.

She'd thought of him constantly these past few weeks. He

was a wonderful father, totally devoted to making her happy. The newspapers said he was a big-time bookie, head of the numbers racket. She feigned ignorance on the matter. She did know people watched their step around him. Jake did. Jake wouldn't have dared to cross her if Daddy were alive. Mom would have taken care of him.

Just thinking back to how she'd discovered her very own rugs in the homes of some of CD's clients sent her into a barrage of profanity. Actually her cussing vocabulary was so limited that she was quickly at a loss. She mulled over the situation: Her stolen rugs were all accounted for and (she hoped) stowed safely away. But Detective Hannagan was still in the picture. Sooner or later he'd be on to her. Right now, though, Jake was the problem. She knew in her heart that he was no thief. Then why? Why did he do it? Was he trying to prove something? She'd contemplated life without him, but who was she kidding? She depended on him, leaned on him. Damn it, she needed him.

And he? What did he need? To steal her rugs? So what if the business paid for them? She'd found them. They were hers; it was understood. She hated being so rational. She'd always had the upper hand: the money and the temperament. She liked it that way.

She pondered her problem. It was her call.

She could confront Jake, demand an explanation. Why did he sell her rugs? How did he have the nerve? What had happened to their relationship? Why was she so reluctant to talk; when did she become so dependent?

Doris had plenty of money of her own. Mom had seen to that. She could live independently. In fine style. But Jake kept her focused, kept her from going off the deep end. Life without him would be too hard. And finally, there was, God help her, the real possibility that she still loved him.

Why did Jake allow her to see the rugs he'd shanghaied? Very careless of him. That wasn't like Jake. Was there something wrong with him? Was he having memory lapses? Early onset Alzheimer's? A shiver ran through Doris. It was much easier to be enraged with Jake than to be worried about him. And then it hit her! He *wanted* her to find out! He, of course, knew she'd find out. He took her rugs to show her who was in charge. Like Mom. So she'd respect him. Even to the extent of Mom's terms, illegally. That was going pretty far. Still it made sense to her. "Jake Seagull, you numskull, we've got to talk." Doris felt better immediately.

Unfortunately, there was more to her dilemma. What was to become of her accomplices, those who had done her bidding? She didn't even know their names. Her trusty old special mentor had made all the arrangements. Innocent people would have to take the heat, and it was her fault. In her anger she hadn't thought it through. She was responsible. She'd at least have to get them good lawyers. Would that be enough?

Doris had a splitting headache. Where could she turn? She would dearly love to talk to her secret partner, but he said they had to stay out of contact. They hadn't spoken since the night he'd called to say the deed was done, that all of her rugs were safe and accounted for.

Her immediate reaction then was joy. A pox on Jake. It was a very satisfying moment.

The afterglow hadn't lasted. Her reasoning powers kicked in and she was forced to consider the consequences. Then Mike Hannagan arrived on the scene. What could she expect? Any day now he'd crack the case. She'd have to be brave and take her punishment. "Never complain, never explain"—that was Daddy's motto whenever he was in a tight spot. But then he knew he could afford the high-priced lawyers to get him off. Well, she wasn't poor. She'd better look up his legal team; she was going to need them.

Finally, she hadn't expected business at CD to fall off so dramatically. She hadn't figured on the adverse publicity. Who wanted to buy a rug at the store if it was going to be stolen subsequently? The price for her moment of revenge was going to be dear.

No matter how many times she reviewed her plight, the blame still fell squarely on Jake. It was bizarre. Jake, who had been trying to gain her respect and confidence, imitating her daddy. If he hadn't sold her rugs in the first place, she never would have had to retrieve them. What she'd done was justifiable, but wasn't there a law of unintended consequences . . .

Benny Bloom fell in love with Doris the day she was born. As it happened, the police had Mom, Meyer O. Mintz, in custody that particular Tuesday, so Benny had to pinch-hit for his boss. Ethel had called Ben when her labor pains started. He'd raced to Mom's home in Brookline, bundled Ethel into his car, and broken all speed records getting her to the Beth Israel Hospital.

Doris was born seven hours later. She was a beauty. Tears came to Benny's eyes when they held up the tiny, perfect baby. He'd wasted no time delivering the happy news to Mom, who was temporarily detained at the local jail. Mom was out the next day, but he'd missed the blessed event, for which Ethel never forgave him. She didn't much like her husband's line of work anyway.

It was a big operation, the numbers racket in the northeast and Meyer O. Mintz was the undisputed kingpin. Mom ran a tight shop; Benny Bloom was his right-hand man. They'd been together a long time. Mom was a father figure to Benny even though there was only a ten-year age discrepancy.

Benny Bloom's real parents had been Russian immigrants. They'd come to America separately, seeking freedom and, perhaps, their fortunes. They'd met and married in Boston. Benny was born one year later. Freedom they found, but times were hard and the streets were not paved with gold. They'd sought out long-lost relatives who'd found them work and a place to live. Benny's father helped out at a kosher butcher shop. At night he brought home the discarded meat scraps to Minnie, his wife, who cooked them up with carrots, potatoes, and onions in a big, black pot that always sat on the stove. There wasn't much variety in their diet, but they always had food on their table.

When Benny turned five, he was sent to school. Never had there been such a scholar! In the first grade he won every academic prize, same thing in the second, again in the third and fourth. His parents could hardly believe they had produced such a genius. Benny was the joy of their lives.

What's more, he was growing into a fine-looking boy. Tall for his age, strong, and well-coordinated, he was the star of the rough-and-tumble schoolyard games. After school he didn't have much time. He was busy earning money. He ran errands for the butcher, bussed tables at the Waldorf Cafeteria, swept up at Billy Schwartz's Men's Store. He loved the jingle of coins in his pocket and bringing home money to his mother. She protested but he knew it helped.

Then tragedy struck. One balmy Shabbas afternoon in spring, his parents, who rarely had time to relax, were taking a little fresh air in their neighborhood. As they walked arm in arm on Blue Hill Avenue, a runaway trolley car jumped the track, and they were killed instantly. Benny was an orphan at eleven.

A kindly distant cousin took him in. It was a roof over his head, but the unheated, cold-water flat was not to Benny's liking. Whether it was expected of him or not, he felt he had to pay his way. So he hustled a little harder after school, always keeping some small change for himself. At the minimum, he needed a nickel to pay for his weekly shower and towel at the Upton Gym. He kept himself neat and clean. His mother would have been proud.

After a particularly frigid, bone-chilling winter with his relatives, he decided he had to move. The kitchen stove, which gave off some heat, was not on his side of the apartment. Ben's room was like an icebox. He found himself a room in a heated tenement and vowed never to look back.

Now he needed serious money. He had to pay for his room plus his nightly fifty-cent dinners at Slovin's Hungarian Restaurant. Mr. Slovin was very nice to Benny. He kept an eye on him, encouraging him to do his homework at the restaurant after hours. It was the only chance he had.

Benny qualified for Boys Latin School, a golden opportunity for poor boys with top grades. College scholarships were often awarded to the most promising students. Mr. Slovin urged Benny to go to Boys Latin even though the courses would be tougher, which meant a lot more work. Ben hesitated. He was already a very busy young man.

He did go to Boys Latin, but not for long. What happened was that he met an older boy at the Upton Gym who seemed to know the score. Eddy wore sharp clothes and always had a wad of folding money in his pocket. For thirty-five dollars he would get Benny set up in the shoeshine business, maybe even find him a spot at Suffolk Downs, the new race track in East Boston.

Benny had never been to a horse race, didn't know anyone who had. It wasn't a Jewish thing, he thought, but where better to make money than from people who were throwing it away? He saw the light and agreed to pay Eddy the thirty-five dollars for the necessary supplies and a quick course in shoe maintenance. To this day, Benny believed that hard-earned thirty-five-dollar investment was the smartest move he'd ever made.

Because that was where he met Mom. At Suffolk Downs. Mom loved the horses, couldn't get his fill. As a young man he liked nothing better than spending the afternoon at the track. He had a brain like a supercomputer. Calculating odds was child's play to him. He was usually a big winner. Feeling flush, he often stopped at Benny's corner for a shoe shine.

Somewhat of a dandy, he enjoyed the vigorous shoe buffing and the complimentary whisk-broom once-over that Ben had incorporated into his service. Besides that, he liked Benny's easy manner and courteous attitude.

One thing they didn't agree about was the horses. Meyer considered racing the sport of kings. Ben, who spent his few spare minutes at the track visiting the stables, also loved the horses, but felt the magnificent animals with their rippling muscles and sleek, velvety coats were badly misused. Imagine breeding horses to carry half a ton of thoroughbred flesh on delicate little ankles! It was a sin. No wonder there were so many spills and so many horses having to be put down.

It was a new slant on horses for Meyer. He didn't agree but he respected Benny for standing up to him. The kid had spunk. He could use a smart young man in his organization. He spent time talking and kidding with Benny whenever he was at Suffolk Downs. He was a big tipper too. Benny was flattered by the attention from a sophisticated, older man. Neither one could fathom only a ten-year age difference. Meyer thought Ben older by far than his sixteen years; Ben gave the twenty-six year-old Meyer another decade.

After Ben told Meyer his family history and the fact that he had no close kin, Meyer was hooked. He would make Ben family. And so he did. As Mom put together his power base, Ben worked along with him. Mom wrested each operation into the fold. Ben gave him the support he required by threatening, by intimidation, by strong-arming, by whatever was necessary. Meyer was grateful, which made Benny happy. Plus the money was rolling in.

The boy who thought horse racing a sin found he had no problem operating just south of the law. Mom needed him, was good to him. That was enough for Ben. He'd found a *home.*

Once Doris was born, Benny was hopeless. He couldn't tear himself away from the little darling. He hovered over her as a baby, dandled her on his knee as a toddler, helped her with her schoolwork when she was a little girl. He was indispensable to her. She loved her doting, good-natured Uncle Benny. Who wouldn't? In his eyes she could do no wrong. No one else, except her own daddy, treated her as if she were a real, live princess. They both called her that, their Princess. She came to expect and rely on their unconditional homage.

It was a tough act to follow. Ethel, her mother, a nice, sensible woman, tried to instill a sense of perspective in her daughter. She didn't have much luck, thanks to Doris's two fondest admirers.

When Doris entered her teens, there was a big change. As a student at Beaver Country Day School, a prestigious private prep school, she began to see things in a different light. Her peer group set the standards. She didn't like or want Uncle Benny at her house all the time. She had a hard enough time explaining her father to her new chums, who, it seemed, were begat by doctors, lawyers, bankers, and business tycoons.

Banished from his favorite habitat, Benny decided it was time for a family of his own. He'd had his eye on a pretty telephone operator at Suffolk Downs, Belle Wirewrack. She liked him too. Soon they were married. Mark Elliot, their son, was born ten months later.

Benny was in heaven. Mom was delighted for Benny. He showered the newlyweds with gifts and, when Mark was born, opened a bank account for the little fellow with a handsome first deposit. Everyone was overjoyed.

Except for Doris. She supposed Uncle Benny wouldn't have time for her now. The fact that she hadn't had time for him in a long, long while tended to slip her mind. She obviously took a dim view of the joyful proceedings. Benny understood. He made a point to see her and to reassure her that she would always be his Princess. And through all of her life, in good times and in bad, Uncle Ben had been there for her. More often than not, Doris took his unswerving devotion as her due, and often treated him in a cavalier fashion. But Benny Bloom stood firm, to the despair of his wife Belle and his son Mark, who never cottoned to Doris's highfalutin ways.

When Mom passed away, Doris insisted on having Uncle

Benny at her side. Only he would do. It was a toss-up as to which one of them was more distraught. During the funeral week, she spent long hours talking to Ben about her father. He listened to her patiently, and that seemed to assuage her grief. It helped Benny too. Poor Ethel, who was also very sad, was left out in the cold. Doris hardly spoke to her mother.

Years before he died, Mom had cleaned up his act. Which was when he'd set up the G & L Transportation Company for Benny. Both men retained their zest for the sly double deal and the canny cover-up, but times had changed, and they were determined to stay abreast. What they wanted was something to do. Mom was going to try his hand in the stock market; he thought Ben would like the trucking business. They were still very close. They saw each other constantly, and they made it a point to keep in touch with their former cohorts, for old times' sake.

There was plenty of money. Mom had been very astute with his investments, despite his penchant for the horses. He'd made Benny a rich man along the way. Benny had no complaints. It was his son Mark who insisted on doing business to the letter of the law. Where did he come from? Benny often wondered.

When Ben received that odd call from Doris, he didn't hesitate for one minute. She was very upset, and she needed a big favor, a really big favor. She explained the situation and told him what she wanted.

"Princess, I'll take care of everything. Don't you worry your pretty head," he'd said without missing a beat.

And he had. He'd done what she'd asked. Clean as a whistle. Not a trace, not a clue. He still had the touch. As far as Benny was concerned, the case was closed.

Truthfully, nothing made Benny happier than indulging his Princess. If his son would only relax a bit. Was that too much to ask?

Make no waves, that was Mark Bloom's motto. The only offspring of the flashy Benny Bloom, he had learned to walk the middle ground, to moderate his behavior.

Whereas his father basked in the glow of appreciation and approbation, Mark went the other route. He'd spent the better part of his life avoiding the limelight. Once he understood what Benny was about, he headed in the opposite direction. He was a puzzlement to his fun-loving parent, this sober, conservative son. And it was rough going for Mark. Only Belle, his mother, understood. She'd learned how to deal with Benny, no matter what.

Actually Mark Bloom was a very nice person, reasonable in every respect except on the subject of his father. He was married to a lovely woman with whom he had fathered two adorable daughters. They lived in a comfortable old house in the town of Brookline, where they were active in school and town affairs. Mark himself shunned publicity, as expected.

It was a case of too much, too soon, growing up with Benny Bloom. Overload was the problem. Mark was gifted with every toy in the catalogue. His closet was crammed with clothes. Benny couldn't walk into his home at night without a gift or treat for his son. From the beginning, the little boy was bewildered by the endless supply of stuffed animals and playthings. He loved his teddy bear, but that was the extent of it. Clutching Teddy, he watched with huge eyes as the staggering array of toys piled up. He just couldn't deal with it.

Benny, on the other hand, got a big kick out of all of it. He played with the blocks and spinning tops, with toy soldiers and jacks-in-the-box, with the swings and games and trains, the paraphernalia he had missed as a child. He didn't understand his son's attitude. With his natural enthusiasm, he tried to lure Mark into the world of make-believe. Unsuccessfully. His son looked on from the sidelines.

The only other small child in Benny's experience was Doris. She had loved every toy and plaything she was offered. She never had enough. She'd rip off wrapping paper and shriek with delight at each new wonder. It was a treat to see her react. Not so with Mark. He wasn't a disappointment, he just wasn't much fun.

At school Mark was a good student; his grades were respectable if not top-notch. At sports he was a team player, not a star. He knew how to get along. Throughout his school years, he kept the same low profile.

He loved college. The University of Michigan was far enough away from Boston that nobody there had ever heard of Mom or of his chief henchman, Benny Bloom. When his father came to visit, he was just another doting parent lost in the crowd. The years at Ann Arbor were some of Mark's happiest.

Mark made his biggest mistake after graduation. He let his father talk him out of law school. Benny didn't think too highly of the legal profession. Mom had set up the trucking company for Ben. The potential was obvious, but the daily grind, the endless routine, was not Benny's style. He needed a smart, well-organized manager, a person he could trust. He needed his son.

When Benny wanted something, he could be very persuasive. He dangled a luxurious apartment with carte blanche furnishings, a membership in any health club in Boston, a sports car, foreign or domestic, and an exorbitant salary with regular, guaranteed increments. If that wasn't enough, Mark would be his own boss. What more could anyone want?

Mark didn't know. Deep down in his heart, he probably had misgivings, but at twenty-one, could anyone resist such temptations?

And Mark enjoyed putting the business to rights. It took great effort, all of his organizational skills. Benny had staffed the place with old pals who behaved as if it were their clubhouse. On a typical day, they played cards and the horses while dispatching plum jobs to their friends and relatives. Nepotism was alive and well at G & L. And when Benny dropped in, it was party time.

Things changed when Mark took over. Having given his son a free hand at G & L, Benny had to abide by the new rules. Rule Number One: his buddies had to go, no ifs, ands, or buts. They grumbled at being uprooted but left peaceably. Benny found them other cushy jobs. He knew everybody, and everybody wanted Benny to be happy. He had been a powerful figure in his day. And a popular one.

So Mark went to work. His goal was to make G & L Transportation one of the finest trucking companies in the business. It took time. He put together a professional, hardworking administrative team. His vehicles were fairly new and not in bad condition. He had them put in tip-top shape and bought more. All drivers were replaced. The new standards were stringent and absolute. Mark paid for and expected the best from his new truck drivers. Every once in a while Benny came up with a qualified trucker whom Mark felt obliged to take on. Not often.

Mark studied the competition. Whatever they were doing, he tried to do better. His equipment was up to date and clean. His people were reliable and courteous. A well-thought-out advertising campaign got his message across. The wheels started to roll. Mark had to expand the routes by popular demand.

Every day Benny stopped in for a few minutes. His visits were less and less disruptive; he knew so few of the people. Still, he enjoyed having a place to go. It gave shape to his day. For many years on Mondays, Wednesdays, and Thursdays, he had breakfasted with Mom and two or three of their old cronies at Moe's Place, a well-known, established deli in Brookline. It was a ritual. They talked about the good old days. If they did a little business on the side, it wasn't serious. The IRS was ever alert to these senior citizens. One or more of them was always under scrutiny, being audited. They grumbled a lot.

Benny liked to say he had to go to work. Mark always made time for him. He went over the day's schedule with him, quoted the latest hauling rates, repeated the industry scuttlebutt. Benny wasn't really interested; he pretended. Mark knew, but out of deference he played the game.

The years passed. G & L grew to be a giant in its field. If Mark had any misgivings about the business, it didn't show. He worked hard and was well respected.

With Mom's death, Benny became a different person. He was quieter, his abundant vitality diminished, his flashy clothes toned down. He focused on his temple and Jewish charities. He adopted the persona of a philanthropist.

Mark knew that Benny kept in touch with Mom's family. Mark never could stand Princess Doris. Such a snob! Her mother was a pleasant woman, but the uppity Doris with her fancy rug store and manner got to him. The story in the *Globe* about the rug thefts and their connection to the Princess' store caught his eye. Strange. She must be in a snit. He didn't wish her any harm, but the thought of Doris getting her comeuppance was not unpleasant.

This day Mark was in his office reviewing the recent scheduling, which appeared to be in order. Why, then, was a detective nosing about? Mark kept a sharp eye on every aspect of the business. He was on a first-name basis with each trucker.

True, his father still had two or three loyal cohorts on line, but they were due to be phased out soon. At the back of his head there was a nagging thought that Benny just might have pulled a fast one. A fast one on his own son? Mark didn't know what to think or where to look. He needed to talk to Benny, straight talk. He hadn't worked his butt off for the last twenty years to have his own father muck up a damn fine business in a nostalgic burst of wrongdoing.

Mark let out a long, low sigh. It never stopped, he thought. All of my life I've had to contend with a lovable, crooked father. How did I get suckered into thinking of him as a pillar of his temple, a veritable humanitarian? He hadn't changed. He'd deny everything. Mark knew it. Why bother? He'd have to get to the bottom of this himself. Mark picked up the phone and asked for his general manager.

Twenty minutes later, Mark, his head in his hands, was trying to make sense of some unpleasant and unwelcome information. He was in a sweat. He groaned. "This can't be happening. It's a nightmare. I'll wake up soon. He's an old man. Once a crook, always a crook. He's going to jail this time. They'll throw away the key. And we'll be out of business."

Mark was so conflicted with worry and anger and concern for Benny that he couldn't think. He was having a hard time processing the facts. Tony and John, the bozos; had taken one of G & L's trucks. To do what? Mark didn't want to know. Yes, he did. Who authorized it? How did they come to Benny? They were young guys, not even his generation. Who had the truck repainted? Who was in charge here anyway? Where was Benny? Mark picked up the phone again.

Benny was attending a meeting at his beloved Temple Beth Am in Brookline. The nominating committee of the board of trustees had just called it quits. The meeting had been long and tedious. Finally they had a slate of officers for the upcoming year. It was uphill work trying to find qualified people to serve. Not a popular pastime these days. Once again, Benny Bloom's persuasive powers had saved the day. Everyone was appreciative.

Benny himself was in a jovial mood. Mission accomplished. He felt good. He was due at G & L about now but decided not to hurry. He would take a leisurely stroll down Beacon Street. It was a beautiful day, warm and sunny. The sky was bright blue with occasional puffs of cottony clouds.

He walked slowly. He wasn't as spry as he used to be. On the other hand he didn't need a cane or a crutch like some of the old geezers at the temple. Not yet. He reflected on his life in general. I'm one lucky s.o.b., he concluded.

As he ambled past the Planned Parenthood clinic at 1031 Beacon Street, the action speeded up. A young man, a nylon stocking pulled down over his head, grotesquely distorting his features, came running out of the building brandishing a semi-automatic. He ran directly into Benny, who without a thought, in a reflex motion, grabbed for the gun. The old man elbowed the stunned gunman in the chest, the weapon went off, and the two men fell to the sidewalk in a spatter of blood.

Inside the clinic, two women were dead by the hand of the killer, who now lay pinned beneath the body of Benny Bloom. One woman was a dedicated and beloved social worker, the other, a brilliant and caring young doctor. Outside Benny was hurt—how seriously was not clear. The gunman, momentarily knocked unconscious as his head hit the concrete walk, would prove to be relatively unscathed.

A crowd gathered. There were several witnesses to Benny's heroic act. The police arrived, then the ambulances. Benny was carted off to the Beth Israel Hospital. He was sent up to surgery immediately. His surgical team worked quickly and precisely. The damage was repaired. Now it was touch and go.

Could the tough old man survive?

◆ ◆ ◆

The story hit the afternoon papers. Due to the nature of the killings, UPI and AP were having a field day. Benny Bloom was a national hero. Even the right-to-lifers had to recognize a hero. The hospital was teeming with newspeople waiting to interview Benny, who was now fighting for his life in the Intensive Care Unit.

Ten miles away in Wellesley, Doris had just glanced at the front page of the *Globe*. As she scanned the story, she started to moan. It couldn't be true, it couldn't be! Uncle Ben was her rock of Gibraltar. He couldn't die. She had to get to the Beth Israel Hospital.

It was her first instinct. Her hands were shaking so badly that she couldn't write a note for Jake. She picked up the phone to dial the store, but her trembling made that impossible too. She groped for her car keys and, finding them, rushed out to her car. There was a problem unlocking the door. As she struggled with it, Jake, arriving home early from work, managed to block the driveway with his big, gray van.

"Get out of my way! Jake, move the *car*! *Please*."

Jake did as he was told, narrowly missing a collision. Doris barreled out of the driveway, careened onto the street, and zoomed off in a swirl of dust.

"Where does she think she's going? If she doesn't kill herself or some innocent bystanders first, she'll be pulled in by the police," he grumbled.

Jake picked up the newspaper she'd dropped on the ground, looked at it curiously, and with a sigh, headed back to his van. He thought he knew what was on his wife's mind. At least he knew where she was going.

The waiting room at the hospital was crowded. Mark Bloom and his mother Belle sat close together on a dark green vinyl sofa, besieged by a noisy pack of photographers and reporters.

"We have nothing to say. We're waiting, that's all. Please have the decency to leave us alone." A flash went off, and another picture of the distraught Bloom family went on record. Mild-mannered Mark was reaching the end of his tether. Only his mother's firm grip on his arm kept him in rein.

"Don't lose your temper," she whispered under her breath. "They'd love a picture of us wild-eyed and hysterical."

Mark was well aware that if they checked the files on Benny, it was all over. He wasn't going to give them cause. Having spent the morning delving into the old man's Oriental rug caper, he was almost stupefied by the latest turn of events. The single thought in his mind: Please, God, let him live, let my father live!

At this moment Doris burst into the waiting room. "How's Uncle Benny? Where is he? I have to see him." She ran over to Mark. He got up and braced himself as she threw herself into his arms. She was sobbing.

"Sorry, Doris, no one is allowed to see him. We've been here all afternoon. The doctor said he'd let us know if he comes to. Mother and I are the designated visitors, nobody else."

"You don't understand," she insisted, "I have to see him. It's very important."

Without a word to Belle, she slumped into a nearby chair. She didn't recognize or feel the antagonism emanating from the Blooms, mother and son. They did not like Doris. She knew that. Why was she here?

Mark knew the answer, but he was too upset for it to register. Belle had no clue. The long wait continued.

The following morning at Classic Design was typical of the transitional period at the store. Jon had given notice. Three weeks. He showed up for work each day, but that was about it. His mind was elsewhere. The women were surprised and pleased to hear of his new venture, but sad to think of his leaving. They were a closely knit group, and he would be missed. They were planning a farewell party for him. It was a bittersweet time.

At the moment they were huddled around the desks, reading the headline feature in the *Globe:* the murders at the Planned Parenthood clinic. Sophie reminded them of the connection between the brave old man who captured the killer, and Doris Seagull.

"She's going to be very upset. She calls him Uncle Benny. He's not a blood relation; I'm not sure what the connection is."

"What a nifty old guy," said Sarah. "Imagine, at his age, tackling a kid with a gun! He did the Boston PD a real service. He deserves a medal. I wonder if the FBI will get involved. I must ask Mike."

Lesley was quietly outraged by the stupid, needless killings.

She had often thought of volunteering in some capacity at the Planned Parenthood clinic. If the right-to-lifers meant to frighten people away, this would do it. The gunman must be a lunatic. A woman was entitled to an abortion if she wanted one. It was the law of the land, but for how much longer? Lesley wondered. She really had to join the fight for women's rights, to stand up and be counted. Time—where would she find the time?

"It's maddening to sit here. I'd like to do something, show I support Planned Parenthood. What can I do?" Sarah asked no one in particular.

The phone rang; Jake calling. Off schedule. He said that he and Doris were at the hospital with the Bloom family, that they'd spent the night in the waiting room, and that there'd been no change. "Anything doing at the store?"

Sophie updated him and assured him that all was well, not to worry. She asked him to keep them posted.

"That's interesting! I didn't know the Seagulls and the Blooms were so close," said Sophie thoughtfully.

The phone again, this time for Lesley. It was Peter, and he wanted to see her. Not today. No way. As tactfully as she knew how, she attempted to explain. He tried to entice her; Lesley couldn't be budged. "Another time," she said distractedly.

Peter hung up the phone and drew a deep breath. He knew, whatever the reason, their time together was playing itself out. Lesley, his lady of the magic carpets, had given him a new lease on life. Damn the cliché! That's how he felt. What a woman, what a glorious woman! Well, it wasn't over yet, not by a long shot. He had to comfort himself with that thought.

Thinking of Peter, Lesley was struck by her own attitude. She couldn't be at his beck and call whenever he felt the urge. There were only twenty-four hours in a day. Why shouldn't *she* say when? Don't be ridiculous, she scolded herself. Having an affair is a sneaky, lowdown business for a reasonably happily married woman. So take what time you can!

Don't spoil your own show. She was feeling tuckered out, that was the problem. If she were younger or stronger or less introspective, she could probably juggle two lives indefinitely. Fingering her smooth, lustrous pearls, which she loved dearly and wore constantly, she mulled over the situation. She couldn't help smiling.

What about the Planned Parenthood clinic? Her intentions were good, but when would she find the time to volunteer? If she didn't support the cause, what right did she have to criticize? As it was, she had trouble with the basics, like keeping herself in meticulous order. It was a damned nuisance. But as long as she was appearing in the buff, she had to keep her legs shaved, her toenails polished, her upper lip bleached. She had to exercise and diet and remember to hold in her stomach. Her lingerie had to be lacy and new, her pantyhose without a snag. Her clothes spent as much time in the cleaners as they did in her closet. Her curly locks were coifed and trimmed on a regular basis. She douched once a week and saw her gynecologist semiannually. It was exhausting. There was much to be said for a comfortable old husband.

An attractive young couple, similarly attired in jeans and black leather jackets, entered the store. They gazed at the rugs hanging on the walls, then looked quizzically over at the desks. Sarah got up. Jon joined her from somewhere in the back.

"Would you like some help?" Sarah asked perfunctorily.

"We need all the help we can get. We've decided on Oriental rugs for our new digs in Cambridge, and we're here to do business. How do we start?"

"Do you have a floor plan or room measurements?"

"We do. It's all here in the blueprints."

They unrolled their floor plan and laid it flat on a pile of rugs. Sarah and Jon settled down to study the layout of a large condominium—one of five, they were told, carved out of an abandoned church. They commented on the unusual and innovative use of the space. As they chatted with the couple, Sarah and Jon both got the distinct impression that money was no object, that getting the apartment right was their goal, and as soon as possible.

The show commenced. A lovely mellow Herez, the perfect fit for the living room area, elicited nods of approval from Kara and Dan Miller. A good start. For their large dining alcove, they wavered between an interesting semi-antique Bakhtiari and a fine old Senneh. They were intrigued by the Senneh, by its dense but subtle design of almond-shaped roses on the pale wool background, even though Sarah told them that the thin kilim would be a problem in a well-trafficked eating area. They decided to try both. A handsome Tekke carpet of the Bokhara family was an easy favorite for the television corner. So far, so good.

Unaccustomed as they were to snap decisions at CD, Sarah and Jon were getting a little giddy. With some strenuous help from the boys in the back, they rolled out a few more of their best. The Millers fell in love with a soft, salmony pink Sarouk for their bedroom. For the smaller spaces, the foyer and the hall, they chose a bold Kazak and a compatible Shirvan. The flattened star medallions of the Shirvan on its deep blue field was dynamite with the Kazak. The two Caucasian rugs were made for each other. Good show! And for the final touch, they wanted one small perfect rug at the entranceway as a welcoming harbinger to their domicile.

But here they hit a snag. They couldn't find a rug they loved in the size they needed. The Millers were disappointed; they wanted the whole works. Sarah and Jon assured them they would find the perfect rug. In the meantime, why not try the others? They agreed.

Arrangements were made to deliver the impressive pile of rugs. Sarah took an imprint of their American Express card to secure the temporary loan of the merchandise. No, Dan Miller insisted upon a detailed tally plus the tax and wrote a check for the full amount. If the sale went through, it would be a record-breaker for Classic Design. The Millers left with many thanks.

Sarah and Jon had always worked well together. Today

they'd hit a new high. Jon viewed it as a bang-up finish to his career at CD. Sophie and Lesley were impressed and congratulated the two. Sophie didn't know how Jake would be able to replace Jon and, probably, Sarah. Why Sarah was lingering at CD was a mystery. She had her freedom and millions of dollars to pave the way. It was time for her to try her wings, to go for it.

The phone interrupted her train of thought. Jake had bad news. Benny Bloom was dead. Jake and Doris were still at the hospital. She was in a state of shock. They might go home or they might come to the store, depending on Doris. He didn't know; he'd be in touch. He hung up abruptly, before Sophie could tell him of the big sale.

They were appalled by the news. They had no idea that courageous old Benny had any connection to CD other than being a foster uncle to Doris. They discussed the implications of the murders.

"Maybe Cardinal Law's moratorium on abortion rights protests will cool things off, maybe not. There are plenty of crazies in this world," said Sarah.

"One of these days the Supreme Court is going to reverse its Roe *v.* Wade decision, and we'll be back to square one: women dying from messy, back alley abortions," pronounced Lesley grimly.

"God forbid," intoned Sophie.

# 30

Doris had fallen apart. Sobbing, she refused to leave the hospital waiting room. Jake didn't know what to do. Mark and Belle were down the hall saying their last goodbyes to Benny. Doris and Jake were alone.

"Doris, honey, it's all right. I'm here with you. Benny enjoyed his life. He had good years and died a hero."

Doris was despondent, in more ways than one. Nothing Jake said registered. She'd badly wanted to see her beloved Uncle Benny before he died. She had to ask him where he'd stashed the rugs. Where were they hidden? Everybody was against her: the doctors, the nurses, Mark and Belle, even Jake. They wouldn't let her see him, and now it was too late. Of course she was upset by his death, but . . .

Jake was beginning to think he needed help. Doris was frightening him. Her frenzy of grief seemed over the edge. She wasn't all *that* fond of Benny. Of that Jake was certain. What was going on?

A nurse, alarmed by the commotion, entered the waiting room. Jake motioned to her. He explained quietly that his wife had just lost her favorite uncle and that perhaps she needed a sedative. Would there be a doctor to see her?

An hour later Jake was driving his wife home. They had left her car in the hospital garage. Doris was silent and subdued, occasionally dabbing at her eyes with a tissue. She was very tired. She had something to tell Jake but couldn't remember what. The medication given to her by the resident was taking effect. All she could think about was her big, warm, comfortable bed.

At the hospital Karen Beth, Mark's wife, was comforting her mother-in-law. She was trying to convince Belle to come home with her. The children adored their grandma, and they would be a welcome distraction.

Mark was making the funeral arrangements from the hospital. He'd been given the use of a small, private office. Detective Mike Hannagan was standing by, waiting to question Benny Bloom's heir apparent. He had some tough questions for him.

Hannagan couldn't help hearing the ruckus in the waiting area. He poked his head in. That it was Doris Seagull surprised him somewhat. But it put things in perspective and finally tidied up the pieces of one puzzle he'd been working. About time.

After the shooting at the clinic yesterday, Hannagan had read the police files on Benny Bloom. Mighty interesting reading. A longtime associate of Meyer O. Mintz ("Mom"), his right arm really, Benny Bloom had spent much of his career one step ahead of the law. The police had picked him up a number of times, but he had never been convicted of, or served time for, any crime. No charges ever stuck. The man had smarts and good legal connections. Apparently he was also a brave s.o.b. He'd proved that yesterday.

When Mark got off the phone, he motioned Hannagan to the chair by the desk he was using. He took a deep breath and waited for the detective to begin. The events leading up to this encounter were so fresh and raw that Mark hadn't had time to feel the pain. Later. Now he'd like to make a deal; he had to make a deal. Much depended on the next few minutes.

For starters, Mike advised Mark that the President of the

United States was planning an official commendation in honor of his father's heroic action, and that he or his mother would receive it posthumously. If they were interested in a White House ceremony, the president would consider it a privilege to hand the certificate to a member of the family. Mark should think about it.

Mark was flabbergasted. All of his life, he'd considered his unconventional, affable father an embarrassment, a thorn. Now this. He had to speak frankly to Hannagan. He hated to do it under the circumstances, but . . .

When he'd finished his tale of intrigue, he asked Mike if he still thought the president would want to commend Benny. Hannagan looked thoughtful. He scratched his head, then smiled.

"You betcha. You'll have to take responsibility for the drivers of the truck involved in stealing the rugs, and if they have no previous criminal record, I'll see if probation with community service can be arranged. That might do it. You say their fathers were close pals of Benny Bloom? Second-generation loyalty. Your dad must have been one helluva guy."

Mark could hardly believe his ears. His father Benny Bloom, being praised, being singled out by the President. Took some getting used to.

"The last hitch is Doris Seagull. That's where the buck stops. Why? What's her angle? Do you know?" asked Mike.

"No, I don't. My drivers, John and Tony, don't even know her name. She has some nerve showing up here at the hospital. You should have heard her carrying on. I admit I can't stand the woman, never could. But she's in the rug business, and my father would do, did do, *anything* she asked. He was crazy about her. He didn't know or care about Oriental rugs—he cared about her."

Mike nodded. "I know. I heard. She seems about to break."

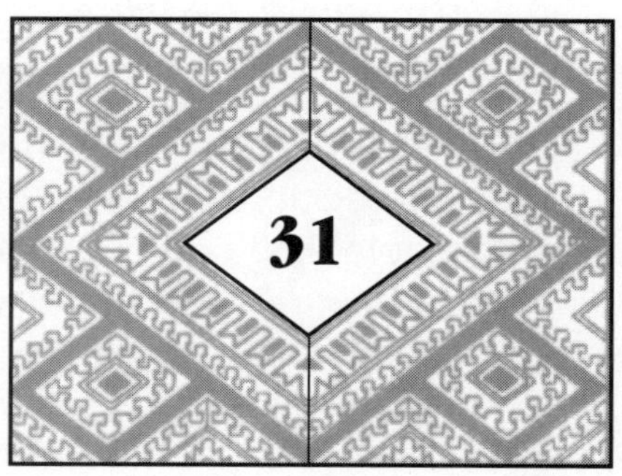

# 31

Jake was slouched in front of the TV staring blankly at the screen. A baseball game, the Red Sox vs. Cleveland, was in progress. Usually an avid fan, today he couldn't concentrate. He was waiting for his wife to wake up. He was straining for a sound from upstairs. A feeling of impending disaster had settled in his gut.

He kept going over the bizarre events of the last thirty-six hours. No matter how he shuffled the cards, one thing seemed clear. Doris was having a breakdown, a serious breakdown. Maybe she'd already had it. Poor Doris, what could he do for her?

The sound of water running in the bathroom overhead grabbed his attention. He listened for a minute then bounded out of his chair and headed for the stairs. He faltered on the third step, stopped, then continued tentatively to the top. Outside of the master bedroom, he cleared his throat, coughed, then entered purposefully. God Almighty! He was unprepared for the sight that greeted him.

Doris, stark naked, was crouched in a corner. In one hand she was clutching what looked like a cosmetic brush or crayon. With a heavy hand and without benefit of a mirror, she was smearing lipstick or rouge or something in vivid patches over her cheeks and brow. She looked down the length of her body and began to decorate the rest of herself in a primitive design that looked oddly familiar to Jake. At first he couldn't think why, then it came to him! She was trying to copy the body painting patterns of a tribe of native Ethiopians. They, she and Jake, had recently watched a National Geographic special highlighting the survival of the Surmas in northern Ethiopia. That was it!

Stopped momentarily, Jake watched her silently. He was treading on dangerous ground.

"Doris, sweetheart, you're getting that stuff on your favorite Kazak. Be careful," he began tentatively.

She looked at him vacantly, then with alarm.

"What am I doing, Jake? What's happening?" She groaned then collapsed in a heap on the floor.

Jake scooped her up and put her gently on the bed. She was crying. He got a big towel and a wet, soapy washcloth and began to clean her off. He worked quickly. His touch was firm. The toweling quieted Doris. He wiped the nipples clean. Doris stirred, opened her eyes, and smiled. An invitation. It was all Jake needed. He was stroking her; she was stroking him. Nice and natural, no devices. She opened herself. Suspended in time, moving slowly, they made love. Never had they felt more attuned, more complete.

Jake was afraid to speak. Life was very strange. *Very,* strange.

Sex, it seemed, was just what Doris needed to calm her and clear her head.

"Jake, that was good, very good, but now it's time to talk. You're not going to enjoy this one bit. I don't know where to start. Hear me out. It's my fault; I'll take the blame. But you're not without guilt. You made me crazy, and I'll tell you how."

Jake listened and listened as Doris spelled out the whole story. Incredulous at first, he soon realized that it was his fault, that he had driven her to desperation. His misguided manipulations of her prized rugs had pushed her over the edge. His plan had backfired. It hadn't made him a hero in her eyes. Just the reverse. He was abjectly sorry. Now they had to figure a way to deal.

"Jake, it's too late. I've got to tell Detective Hannagan. I want to talk to him. No matter what happens next, it has to be better than living in this twilight zone. I at least have to make sure that Uncle Benny's name is cleared in this mess. What's going to happen to his accomplices? They did whatever he asked. *He* did what *I* asked. I went to him because you took my rugs. And sold them! Did you *really* think that would make you some kind of hero with me? Like my father? Are you out of your mind? And to take me to our clients' homes? Jake dear, which one of us is the crazy?"

Hearing a valid and lucid account of her grievances, Jake could only agree. He was accustomed to shielding Doris from the slightest adversity, keeping her from trauma. He'd never allowed her any room for growth on her own. Straight talk might have spared them this nightmare. He should have encouraged change, not kept her on hold. Her autocratic behavior at the store was now a given, take it or leave it. It annoyed the help and the customers, but so what? It was her store, her money. He'd kept an eye on her there, but he had missed the big picture, scrambling for the extra few bucks. He didn't have to sell her rugs. He viewed her collection as an indulgence; she viewed it as a lifetime achievement. Assuming the role of the strong, silent Mom had been a big, fat, stupid mistake. She'd never forgive him. Why should she? Once she told Hannagan the whole story, she could even go to jail. Jesus, what had he done!

"Jake, talk to me, you don't look well. I have to take a shower, and then I'm going to call Hannagan. If I don't do it now, I'll lose my nerve. Promise to stick by me."

"Don't worry, hon, I'll stick like glue. It is my fault. I understand why you did what you did, and I am so sorry, Doris. I promise I'll make it up to you. Somehow, some way."

◆ ◆ ◆

That evening at the Seagulls' home, Mike Hannagan had spent the last two hours closeted in the small, walnut-paneled study with Jake and Doris. He'd listened to the whole story. He'd gone over every detail again and again with Doris. He told her that he knew where her rugs were stashed. She was floored by the news. After a systematic search, Mike had found them at a storage facility in Arlington and had them impounded. The rugs were safe.

"I'll have to give them back, that's all. I'm the rightful owner, but I'll give them back. How?" she asked Mike.

Jake, feeling like a miserable son of a bitch, kept quiet.

"It's not that easy, Mrs. Seagull. A crime has been committed. Several crimes, in fact. Restitution is one thing; retribution is another. The law, that's my job. I don't want to see you behind bars, God knows, but you've deliberately broken the law. No one is above the law."

Even as he spoke, Mike could hear how foolish he sounded. Mrs. Seagull was Mom's daughter. With the example he set, no wonder her peculiar values. Mom got away with murder as did the hero Benny Bloom. Why didn't she contact her fancy lawyers? They'd get her off, no sweat. She wasn't a criminal, she was a victim—Jake Seagull's victim. He, at least, had the grace to look miserable. Mike had to read them their rights and deliver the lecture on justice for all. He was doing his job, but it was getting to him.

He'd been considering a move to the private sector for a long time. A security business—that was the ticket. He knew all the ins and outs. He'd be good at it. For staff, it was a cinch: cops moonlighting in their spare time. Now or never, he thought to himself. Sarah didn't need a worn-out flatfoot in her future. It was time to move on.

That settled in his head, Mike wound up the interview. He arranged for the Seagulls to go down to headquarters the next morning to make their statement. He suggested they bring a lawyer. Seeing that Doris was becoming agitated, he told her that if Bloom's men had no previous record, they could get off with probation and community service. That helped for the moment. Wait until she heard what was in store for her! A smart attorney would have her commit herself for psychiatric observation, at McLean Hospital. McLean was the area's most prestigious mental health facility. There'd be no problem proving her stressed out of her mind. With a bona fide psychiatric report and a hearing before a magistrate, the case could be continued for two years, then dismissed. If fortune smiled on Doris Seagull, all would be forgiven. Still, she was in for some rough sailing, courtesy of her ever loving husband.

At one time Mike had considered law school as a natural segue out of his police job. No longer. He'd seen too much. The fancier the footwork by legal counsel, the more criminals enjoying the better things in life, the less inclined he was to bolt sides. There seemed to be a way around almost any crime. Given the Seagulls' money, and the way of the world, there'd be an out for the missus for sure. That's how it was.

It had been a long day.

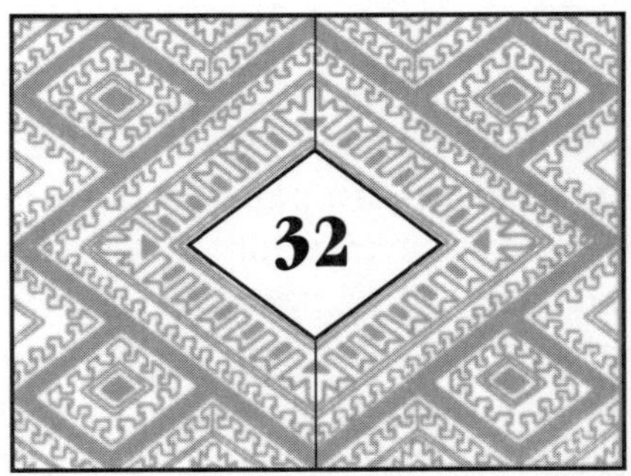

Three weeks later at Classic Design it was business as usual—sort of. Jon was gone. His brand new antique store was scheduled to open in ten days. The mystery of the stolen rugs had been resolved, and the staff was depressed and dismayed. They couldn't believe it. Even the imperturbable Sophie was down in the dumps. Jake came in every couple of days and ghost-walked through the store. His mind was elsewhere, no doubt on Doris, who had been arrested and was temporarily at McLean Hospital. She was in for a twenty-day psychiatric evaluation.

There was a decided hush to the usual chatter. Even so, today Sarah was in an upbeat mood but trying not to let it show. She'd been accepted into the Fine Arts program at Boston University. The official letter was in her shoulder bag. She was excited and so were her kids. They'd been a great source of comfort the past few months. Good kids, solid and yet resilient. She was so proud of them. She'd worried needlessly. Things were going to be okay. She'd have to give notice at CD and that made her sad. She'd stick around until Jake could find a replacement for her.

She hadn't told Mike about Boston U. yet. It was hard to

read him when she talked about her personal goals. A glazed look came over his face. She couldn't figure it. She got really excited when he outlined his plans for a private security company. She assured him it couldn't miss, not with the hazards of today's society, that the timing was perfect. He'd be providing essential services.

Once she had a degree or two, she'd feel more confident. She was sure of that. She'd consider her options when she was ready. Jake had offered to sell her CD the day she'd won the lottery. Perhaps a gallery would better suit her. Who knew what? For Sarah the future beckoned invitingly.

Not so for Lesley. Her double life was running out. She didn't have the stamina for it. So far she'd been lucky; Ken apparently didn't have an inkling. Peter had given her an ultimatum, a deadline. Choose. That she couldn't do. She loved her time with him. And the sex! She hungered for him at all hours of the day and night. It was absurd at her age, but wonderful. At least she had the sense to enjoy it. Still she wasn't willing to trade one reliable, lovable husband for another. Trying to maintain her high-profile, middle-aged body was an endless chore, not to mention trying to keep both her men happy. It was an effort. Anything worth doing was worth doing well, she reminded herself. No wonder she was tired. Savor every lustful encounter, she warned herself. Time is fleeting.

Sophie was just plain depressed. She knew it had to be an inside job. Poor Doris! What a humiliating ordeal. The thought of Doris Seagull going to prison made Sophie shudder. She held Jake equally responsible, no matter the outcome. If he hadn't fooled with her rugs there'd be no problem. He did look and act sincerely conscience-stricken. Doris had felt she was only reclaiming what was rightfully hers. She was, after all, Mom's daughter. Sophie wondered what would become of the store. Jake didn't seem to have the heart for it. So much was pending. She and Lesley could take care of business in the short term, but then what?

◆ ◆ ◆

Jake had hit bottom. He could barely function. Forget business as usual; his mind couldn't contend with the figures in the ledger. Nothing registered. When Sophie summed up the day's events for him, it was as if she were speaking a foreign tongue. Even the rugs in the store looked unfamiliar. He thought only of Doris, Doris shut up in McLean. He was not allowed to see her. They'd never been separated. She needed him; he needed her. It was the same thing. He'd come to realize that she was his life. What a jackass he'd been!

Would she ever forgive him? It *was* his fault, he was responsible. They should be examining his brains, not hers. She hated to sleep alone, she'd be frightened. He knew that. Why couldn't he see her, stay with her? Whatever happened, he would make it up to her. He'd do anything.

And that was what Doris had in mind for Jake. Anything she dreamed up, he'd have to do. Recalling his rather sweet bid for her undivided attention, she was still not planning to make it easy for him. Not for a while. When she wasn't being tested or grilled, she was spending her time at McLean thinking up chores for him. He'd be her househusband in charge of the care and maintenance of their home, which included the cleaning and the cooking. She wondered how long she'd be able to *stand* his cooking. She'd control the TV. The clicker would be out of bounds to Jake. She couldn't decide about the store. She liked the business, but with all the negative publicity she'd be a curiosity, an object of ridicule. Jake, on the other hand, would be the long-suffering husband. Not fair. The store had to go. She'd be a passionate collector of rare Orientals, devoting her time and money to acquiring the most remarkable. She'd travel the world over. Jake would like that.

In the meantime she was behaving exactly as she'd been coached. Her high-priced legal team had set the guidelines. No deviating, they'd warned her again and again. With so much at stake, Doris was toeing the line. Besides, the law firm was costing a fortune. "Money well spent," that's what Mom would have said.

They'd advised her to describe the extreme anxiety she'd experienced at the time of the crimes. And to emphasize the amount of Valium she was taking trying to counteract the stress. They'd urged her to mention the voices that decreed the rugs had to be removed from their wrongful owners, the voices that came in the night and repeated the same thing over and over again. She did as she was told. The psychiatrists were calling the lapse a psychotic episode. They seemed to think she was okay now. Rational enough to stand trial. That was good.

Her legal eagles were working toward a trial without a jury if they could get the prosecution to agree. On the basis of the McLean evaluation, the judge would have to declare her mentally incompetent, temporarily insane at the time of the crimes, and release her. That would be the best scenario.

As for the two drivers, Tony and John, her attorneys were also working out deals for them: two years probation along with a thousand hours of community service to be served in twenty-hour weekly increments. Court costs would be their responsibility, which Doris would gladly pay. If all this came to pass, Doris would be a free woman.

But Jake still needed her attention. She'd choose the cars they'd drive, the restaurants they'd frequent, the friends they'd see. She'd select the sporting events, movies, concerts, and plays they'd attend. Vacations would be her choice. She wasn't sure how long she'd be able to get away with her lopsided regime. She'd pick out his clothes. She never did like his clothes. He'd sport a stylish new haircut despite protest. Sexually, she'd make good use of the devices she'd accumulated. They'd both enjoy that. She smiled in anticipation. Eventually, though, she would forgive him because, bottom line, she loved the silly bastard. He was also essential to her well-being.

◆ ◆ ◆

*Will Doris be deemed mentally competent and stand trial? If so will she be judged temporarily insane and be allowed to go free? If she goes free, what will happen to Jake? Can he handle the rocky road as construed by Doris? For how long?*

*Will there be a happy-ever-after for Sarah and Mike? If his security business flourishes, can he handle a relationship with an independent woman? Once Sarah is established as her own person, will she want to compromise her hard-won status? Will she ever find a fuck as good and as satisfying as Mike?*

*Can Lesley find fulfillment and enough happiness with one man? She'd better. The line forms on the left for Peter's favors, and he's ready and able to bestow the goodies.*

*Will Jon make a success of the antique business? It's what he's always wanted. If so, will Nedra accord him the respect he craves? Will Nedra complete Lives of the Flemish Masters, so important to her academic career? What about Heidi? Can Nedra and Jon attend to business and still make time for their daughter? She's growing up. It won't be easy.*

These questions and more tumbled through Sophie's head as she reflected upon her days at CD. She'd loved her role as Mother Superior. It had been a responsibility, but such a rewarding one. She'd be sad if the store was sold or closed, but that hadn't been decided yet. She didn't know what was going to happen. It was all part of the mystery of life, she thought philosophically. She sighed, opened the ledger, and began to inscribe the day's transactions.

Sophie, it turned out, need not have worried her head. As time and circumstances changed, problems tended to resolve themselves.

Classic Design was no more. In its place stood an elegant Italian knit boutique, Missoni. The space was transformed, unrecognizable. The floor and walls were of gleaming white marble. The few lush and thick area rugs were contemporary in design and wild in color. Small groupings of chairs and settees, upholstered in the primary-colored Missoni fabrics, were scattered about. An ingenious and intricate lighting scheme, strategically placed and spaced, created a luminous, glowing ambiance for the gorgeous, drop-dead merchandise artfully displayed hither and yon in the most tempting fashion. There was not a trace of the former tenant or of those who had attended to its business.

What happened to everyone?

Once Doris was pronounced temporarily insane, set free, and sent home, all hell broke loose. If Jake had any idea of back to business as usual, boy, was he mistaken! Doris decreed Classic Design history, and she wasn't kidding. Jake tried to dissuade her, argued, cajoled, but she wouldn't be budged. She'd had plenty of time to think it through. Jake had to go to his landlord, buy up the rest of his lease (two years to go), and deal with some pretty heavy inventory.

As usual Doris refused any mention of a sale, even the obvious going-out-of-business sale. Not with her carefully chosen rugs! Jake had to dispose of them the best way he could. Doris, of course, had first pick. She took whatever she wanted. Then he put some up for auction; others he placed on consignment. A few he was able to return to his wholesalers. Unbeknownst to Doris, he drastically reduced the prices of any rugs that Sophie, Sarah, Lesley, even Jon, wanted to buy for themselves. It was a once-in-a-lifetime spree, and they went overboard.

Sophie got the Tabriz of her dreams. It was a hunting design with exotic fawn-colored animals roaming the borders of its flowery field. Creamy and light and very elegant. Lesley bought two magnificent Kazaks: one for Peter, one for her own home. Sarah bought for the future, for her children as well as for herself. She bought a Joshaghan, a Herez, a Bakhtiari, and a Saraband. Jon, with a shrewd eye for the antique trade, bought a bundle of small Orientals for Traditions plus a beautiful Sarouk as a birthday present for Nedra.

That was the end of Classic Design. Sophie was beside herself. She'd thought of the store as her own, had loved working there: the problems, the craziness, the responsibility. It was a major part of her life. Halfheartedly she looked for another job, not easy in a downsizing economy. Her references and experience were top-notch, but her age, sixty-three, was against her. She didn't try for long. Soon she wasn't feeling well. Everyone, including Sophie, figured it was a prime case of hypochondria. Too much time on her hands, which was true. Still she felt rotten. A skeptical doctor scheduled her for a battery of tests at a local clinic. The results were grim. Sophie wasn't imagining her aches and pains; she was really sick.

Once the disease was explained to Sophie, she mulled over

the odds, came to terms with her fate, and was subsequently the bravest terminal patient anyone could ever hope for. Her heartbroken family and friends took their cue from Sophie and put on a happy face as they rallied 'round her. She was never alone. Her work family stayed close too. There were errands and chores to be done, transportation to and from treatments to be provided, meals to be cooked and served. But diverting Sophie was the best of all. She was a wonderful audience right to the end. No wonder her devoted circle. There wasn't a dry eye in Temple Israel when Sophie was eulogized, bade adieu, and sent to her eternal rest.

Her former co-workers were in shock. It happened that fast. Perhaps they'd found a modicum of consolation in being with her and in being useful at the end. But no Sophie! It was unthinkable.

Lesley was crushed. She and Sophie had shared so many intimacies. Lesley was not one to bare her innermost self to another human being, but she had come close with Sophie. How she would miss her!

The idyll of Lesley and Peter was also finished. Too many endings. Lesley was collecting unemployment while searching for another job. She wasn't optimistic. She'd had two depressing interviews. She'd been off the job market for a long time. Obsolete and out of step was how she felt.

One fateful day, Ken trying to bolster her morale, insisted she accompany him on a sales trip to St. Louis. She went reluctantly, but the most amazing thing happened. Ken came down with a nasty case of the flu, the full catastrophe: fever, aches, chills. They were stranded at the hotel. Ken was frantic. He had a string of appointments lined up; his sample cases were bulging with the new seasonal merchandise. Could Lesley pinch hit? After all, she'd been selling for years. She wasn't crazy about the idea, but she'd give it a try. Why not? A crash course on his lines in shoes and bags, some vital statistics, and out she went.

Ken had warned she would have trouble getting past the receptionists, that buyers did not take to novices. He was right about the shoe buyers; she didn't get to first base. The good-old-boy system prevailed. But she was a smash in pocketbooks, wrote up more orders in two days than he had chalked up in two years. Go, Lesley!

She was pleased with herself; Ken was dumbfounded. When he'd recovered his health and good sense, he and Lesley sat down together for a strategic powwow. They could work as a team. No more lonely nights on the road. Was Lesley interested? By all means!

After some serious and official negotiating, Lesley got her own line of handbags, totes, and briefcases. Now she and Ken coordinated their selling junkets. Whenever they went on the road, they took care of business, then took time out for themselves. It was a good arrangement. The Kanes were a successful team, so successful that they were featured in a trade magazine. What's more, they were enjoying personal and financial rewards. Lesley and Ken were back in synch.

On a good day Lesley could go eight hours without thinking of Peter.

About Doris and Jake. With Classic Design gone and Jake at loose ends, Doris was calling the shots. She was keeping him busy as planned. He cleaned house and did laundry; he mowed the lawn and did the marketing. He was in charge of the dry cleaning. In his spare time, he acted as her chauffeur. She drew the line at a uniform.

Jake truly believed his treatment was justified, so not a word of protest. His attitude did tend to frustrate Doris, who was looking for a little more interaction.

Jake felt sure that his servitude was finite, that one day Doris would have a change of heart and he would be restored to his former circumstances. He hated to close Classic Design, but he had no choice. The future was the big question mark. Doris was talking about a trip to London. She'd heard about a rare old Tabriz. She'd seen slides and knew it was available. Now she wanted to eyeball it. Jake was hoping that travel would improve his situation. He was counting on it! In the past he'd always taken care of the essentials: itinerary, plane tickets, hotels, everything. Unless Doris was planning a complete about-face he'd regain a measure of authority. She needed him. He was waiting for his chance to prove it.

This time Jake was on target.

Doris was getting sick of the status quo. The humiliation of the tag "temporarily insane," not to mention the endless three weeks spent in the booby hatch (how she referred to McLean) had really thrown her. Daddy never would have allowed it. Jake with his earnest, misdirected bumbling, had made it happen. But enough already! Time was healing the wounds. Doris was in recovery. Sooner or later she'd relent some. The signs were favorable.

The news of Mike and Sarah? They had yet to make their relationship permanent. Both of them had enjoyed some personal highs: She'd earned her bachelor's degree and had almost completed work on her Master of Fine Arts; his security business was booming with branches in five cities to date, which kept him hopping. But their time together was limited and not without problems.

Not sex. Sexually, they were of Olympic gold-medal caliber. They couldn't get enough of each other. They reveled and relished in their lusty appetites. He couldn't keep his hands off of her. She'd gone down on him in more than one semi-public place. It was hair-raising. Considering they could marry, that nothing was stopping them, it was not only embarrassing, it was a matter of contention between them. Mike wanted them to be married. Sarah kept putting him off. She wasn't ready. She loved the aching for him, the fact that he could now make her orgasmic by phone when they were miles apart.

She just didn't want to settle down again. He did. He wanted her in place in a home of their own, taking part in his life, being there for him. He still didn't understand that wasn't going to happen. Sarah needed her own space. Her children had kept her anchored, and she'd loved being a mother, but now it was time to stand back, to watch them spread their wings. It was her turn.

She'd been eyeing a small gallery on Newbury Street. She'd learned that it would be for sale in a year or so. Perfect timing. She was interested enough to have accepted a part-time position there, starting immediately. What better way to check out the possibilities?

Mike thought she had too much on her plate as it was. Between her school work and her kids, and his hectic schedule and his traveling, they had to grasp whatever time together they could. A weekend was a luxury. He wanted more of her. She wanted more of it all. In bed they were well met; out of bed, they were at an impasse. If they could hold on, time, as always, would be the deciding factor. It was still an open chapter.

Sarah had been surprised and pleased at the success of Traditions. It was Jon's baby, and she couldn't be happier. She prayed that a gallery of her own would do as well. She tried, really tried to spend an afternoon a week at Traditions. Jon was already paying off her investment. She was in no hurry. He insisted. Jon was a different person. No more a dilettante or lackey, he was confident and sure of himself, a pleasure to behold. Sarah couldn't get over the change. What a wise, smart move on her part, she often thought to herself. God bless the Massachusetts lottery!

Nedra, the perennial naysayer, wore a big smile these days. She wasn't worrying about paying bills or losing her job or a dependent mate. She was proud of Jon. His expertise in American decorative arts had bowled her over. She had no idea. It had won him a loyal following of serious collectors. Lately at some of the more important American antique auctions, he'd been a contender. Nedra heard no more snide remarks about her youthful husband. Her faculty mates sought him out for opinions or verifications on questionable objets d'art or found treasures. Jon was in great demand at academic get-togethers now.

He loved everything about his new career. And Sarah had made it possible. True friends didn't come any better. Jon was one happy man.

As for daughter Heidi, she was an integral part of Traditions. To their amazement, she'd turned out to be a computer whiz kid. Who would have believed it? She organized and programmed the inventory and kept the accounts, all on the computer. She did this after school and on weekends. They couldn't do without her. She loved being a vital part of the action. She was knowledgeable, courtesy of her father, and well-mannered, courtesy of her mother. Adorable, she owed to both. The customers got a kick out of dealing with Heidi, though they relied on Jon to verify every word of her sales pitch, which annoyed her.

"Sweetheart, you can't expect anyone to part with all that money on the word of a fifteen-year-old. You're doing fine," Jon assured her.

At long last Nedra had the time and the inclination to work on her Flemish masters book; Heidi was busy, happy, and out of trouble; Jon was doing what he'd always wanted; and all their bills were marked paid in full. The Hedstroms were okay.

And that's a wrap for the folks from the unique world of Classic Design, Oriental rug store extraordinaire, now history, but by its staff never to be forgotten.

# Glossary

**Afshar** Although the Afshar is a tribal rug made by nomads living in the area between Shiraz and Kirman (Iran), it has a cotton warp and weft. The reason: the rugs are brought for sale to Kirman, where cotton is readily available. The pile, of course, is wool. One or more diamond-shaped medallions on a field of stylized flowers is a fairly typical design. Deep blue or strong red grounds prevail, always with a small portion of white or cream wool in the pattern. The basic size is five by six feet.

**Azeri** From the mountain area of Eastern Turkey, a coarsely knotted, durable tribal rug, usually of a large, bold diamond pattern in shades of deep blue, red, or rust, and sometimes green on a cream ground. Recently Azeri folk rugs depicting whimsical animals, birds, people, houses, have been successfully introduced to the American market.

**Bakhtiari** Made in about a hundred villages by the nomadic and semi-nomadic people of southwest Persia, the Bakhtiari is easily recognizable. The field is divided into rows of squares, diamonds, or octagons, each one containing a stylized flower, bush, or tree. Rich, dark blue or red backgrounds are typical. Green, gold, and yellow are the usual design colors. Early Bakhtiari rugs had wool warps; today all have cotton warps.

**Bidjar** Extremely durable, called the "iron rug" of Persia, these rugs are woven by Kurdish tribesmen in a small village (Bidjar) in northwestern Iran. The ground colors are dark and rich, usually red, blue or green. Floral designs prevail, sometimes with a central medallion. French-style roses in the borders and in the corners are not uncommon. Bidjars weigh almost twice as much as other Persian rugs due to the high lanolin content of their wool.

**Bokhara (Bukhara)** From western Turkestan (central Asia), traditional carpets, easy to identify: orderly, full-field parallel rows of octagonal guls (also called elephant feet) on a rich red background. Wide, intricate borders are typical. Pakistani Bokharas, popular in America, come in all colors including ivory, tan, brown, navy, and green, as well as in several pastel shades. They are produced in rug factories and are made in a wide range of sizes. There are many wonderful variations of the Bokhara.

**Camel Bag** Resembling a small pile rug with a long woven kilim at one end. The sides are stitched together to form an envelope.

**Flokati** Greek, handwoven woolen rug with a thick, shaggy pile. Typically plain, it is of natural raw wool.

**Gorevan** Rugs from the town of Gorevan in the Herez district are very similar to the Herez but usually of a poorer quality.

**Herez (Heriz)** A thick, coarsely woven, colorful, and tough rug from the district of Herez, located in the northwest corner of Persia. Its warp and weft are cotton. Usually there is a central starlike medallion, always angular, composed of four or eight points on a rusty red background. Other colors used in the Herez are ivory, blue, and yellow. It is an extremely durable rug with innumerable variations.

**Joshaghan** From the village of Joshaghan in central Persia, an easily recognizable knotted wool carpet. The pattern is a regular grid of diamond shapes, much like snowflakes, usually with a diamond medallion at the center. The colors: deep red (the field), dark blue, light blue, and ivory.

**Kazak** The best known and most popular rug of the southern (Russian) Caucasus. The traditional colors are strong reds, blues, greens, and yellows. A typical design includes three aligned medallions with interior smaller decorative motifs. Octagons, hexagons, eight-pointed stars, swastikas, and rectangles are standard geometric shapes found in the Kazak. The weave is coarse but dense, making it very durable. Sizes range from four feet by five feet to eight feet by four and one half feet.

**Kilim** A flat, woven rug. It has no pile and is normally reversible. Some knotted rugs have kilim borders at the top and/or bottom.

**Kirman** Since the sixteenth century, highly sophisticated carpets with well-organized designs have been handwoven in or about the city of Kirman in southern Iran. The wool is generally soft and not hard-wearing. Elaborate floral designs with or without central medallions are typical, although it is not unusual to find Kirmans patterned after French Aubussons. In America, a thick pile rug with a central medallion on an open cream, beige, or white ground is fairly standard. Unlike most Persian carpets, the Kirman continues to evolve in style and fashion to accommodate world trade.

**Malayer** From the region of Malayer in west central Persia, sturdy rugs very similar to the Sarouk although coarser in weave and more geometric in design. The ground color is usually dark blue or rusty red. Scrolling vine borders are common.

**Melas** From southwest Anatolia (Turkey), a prayer rug characterized by its warm colors, ranging from earth tones to gold to brick red. The niche or *mihrab* is usually rust-colored, topped by a pale area containing stylized floral elements. The typical size is three and three-quarter feet by six and one half feet.

**Meshkin** From the Herez area of Iran, Meshkins are

increasingly rare. Typically, the design consists of three octagonal medallions on a semi-open field. Earth tones prevail, and the warp is cotton. They are not made for high-traffic areas. If you can find this handsome rug, it is or should be one of the least expensive rugs of Iran.

**Oriental Rug** A handwoven or hand-knotted one-piece rug or carpet made in the Orient. Normally the term is used to describe the hand-made rugs, traditionally produced in the ancient weaving regions of Persia (Iran), Anatolia (Turkey), Afghanistan, the Caucasus, China, India, Pakistan, the Balkans, and parts of North Africa.

**Saddle Bag** Two small bags similar to a camel bag made in one piece to be hung over the neck of a horse or donkey.

**Saraband** From the mountainous area of central Persia, carpets with an unmistakable design: rows and rows of small *botehs* (pears) from which the paisley motif is derived. There is usually a vine border, and the field of the rug is generally red. The finest example of the Saraband is the Mir. The Saraband is widely copied in India.

**Sarouk** From central Iran, most twentieth-century Sarouks have an all-over floral spray design on a salmony pink field. The village of Sarouk achieves the unusual color with madder roots, dried and pulverized, then soaked in water with yogurt or curdled milk (lactic acid), which creates a dye that gives the wool threads luster, stability, and the desired color.

**Senneh** Made in the town of Sanandaj, formerly Senneh, in western Iran, a very fine handwoven or hand-knotted wool rug. Usually it has an all-over pattern on a blue or white ground with red as the accent color.

**Serapi** Serapi rugs are generally attributed to the town of Serab, which is a part of the Herez district. Many Oriental rug experts insist that the Serapi is in fact a very fine example of a Herez.

**Shirvan** A Caucasian rug from the Shirvan area, now part of Azerbaijan. The design is always geometric, the most common being a tight, repeating pattern of medallions in the shape of flattened stars. The background is either blue or red supporting a wide range of design colors.

**Soumak** Similar to a kilim, a flat (no pile) woven carpet. Unlike the kilim, the weft (side to side) threads in the back hang loose several inches, giving it a shaggy look and making it a heavier, more substantial rug.

**Tabriz** From the second largest city in Persia, carpets of great elegance. The most popular pattern is a central medallion with fractions of equal medallions in the corners. Hunting and vase designs and even prayer rugs are part of the Tabriz repertoire. Its silk prayer rugs are famous. Predominant colors are blue, ivory, brick red, and, more recently, the popular soft pastels.

**Warp** The threads running from top to bottom of any woven material.

**Weft** The threads running from side to side of any woven material.

# • A NOTE ON THE TYPE •

The typeface used in this book is one of many versions of Garamond, a modern homage to—rather than, strictly speaking, a revival of—the celebrated fonts of Claude Garamond (c. 1480–1561), the first founder to produce type on a large scale. Garamond's type was inspired by Francesco Griffo's *De Ætna* type (cut in the 1490s for Venetian printer Aldus Manutius and revived in the 1920s as Bembo), but its letter forms were cleaner and the fit between pieces of type improved. It therefore gave text a more harmonious overall appearance than its predecessors had, becoming the basis of all romans created on the continent for the next two hundred years; it was itself still in use through the eighteenth century. Besides the many "Garamonds" in use today, other typefaces derived from his fonts are Granjon and Sabon (despite their being named after other printers).